HANNIBAL

STARGAZER ALIEN MYSTERY BRIDES #1

TASHA BLACK

13TH STORY PRESS

13th Story Press

PO Box 506

Swarthmore, PA 19081

13thStoryPress@gmail.com

HANNIBAL

1

VIOLET

Violet Locke heard a creak on the stairs.

She looked around quickly, wondering how much evidence she could hide before the maker of the creak arrived.

Spread out on newspaper on the antique handwoven carpet were several beakers of compound, a pair of medical grade scissors, and assorted claws from various animals.

Late morning sun had the scissors gleaming like diamonds. Vi was pretty sure she had started this experiment in the evening. She wondered how long she'd been at it.

But it was too late to figure it out, and too late to clean it up. Someone was already knocking on the door.

"Vi, it's me, I'm coming in," a cheerful voice said.

"Most people knock and then wait for someone to actually invite them in," Vi groused as the door swung open to reveal her landlord.

"Most people answer the door instead of ignoring it," Tony replied tartly, giving her a wink.

He was wearing his favorite smoking jacket, the purple

velvet one. He was also wearing shoes. Normally, he padded up in his slippers to say hello.

"Special occasion?" Vi asked.

"You might say," Tony replied. "How did you know?"

He smiled at her in open anticipation like a child about to watch a magician make a balloon animal. Which was impressive, since Tony had to be in his seventies.

"Just a hunch," Vi said, not wanting to perform like a pony today.

"Oh, come on," Tony said, rubbing his hands together so that his rings clicked. "I love when you do it."

"Fine," she said. "You're wearing your lucky jacket and you have proper shoes on your feet, so I know you're having company. You smell like aftershave but the spicy one not the floral, so I know it's a stranger."

"Incredible," Tony breathed.

"You shaved, which you do every day, impeccably," Vi went on. "But you missed a spot which you never do, so I know you're anxious."

"I missed a spot?" Tony patted his face in horror.

"I would say tax auditor or business opportunity, but I know you don't have any money," Vi noted. "So the tax man won't bother with you. Which means... you're meeting with a potential tenant for the second-floor apartment this morning."

Tony clapped his hands and grinned at her in delight, which made his wrinkles temporarily disappear. For a moment he looked almost like a young version of Al Pacino, then he relaxed his face and looked more like the regular Al Pacino again.

"I am, and this time it's a good one, Vi," Tony said, an edgy look appearing on his face.

"You're going to ask me for a favor," she said warily.

"You know I love you girls," Tony began, and she knew it was bad. "But you can be... a little noisy and unorthodox as neighbors."

Vi nodded and tried not to wince when she spotted the exact moment that Tony noticed the array of animal claws and chemicals on the hand-knotted carpet.

"Anyway," he said, "Micah and I are hoping you and Jana can just kind of... cool it for the next hour, while we show the guy around."

"*Cool it?*" Vi asked.

Vi was incredibly gifted at picking up anything factual. But subtle social stuff wasn't exactly her forte. And "cool it" was exactly the kind of phrase that caused trouble for her.

"No tuba playing, no Nordic vocal exercises, no weird chemical explosions or smells," Tony said carefully.

"We've been very quiet this morning so far," Vi guessed out loud. She definitely hadn't blown anything up.

At just that moment Jana's voice emerged from the bathroom. She was belting out the chorus to *Girls Just Wanna Have Fun*.

"She's got a callback for the Cyndi Lauper Story," Vi explained. "They're going to workshop it at the Public."

"Please, Vi," Tony begged. "We need the money. Sweet Micah misses his cappuccinos."

Tony and Micah were the most romantic couple Vi knew. This was classic Tony, wanting small luxuries for Micah more than he wanted anything for himself.

He was a good man. And a great landlord.

"Fine," Vi said. "Fine, fine. I'll tell her. We'll stay quiet."

"Thank you," Tony said with his usual warm smile. "Now, do I want to know what's going on here?"

He gestured at the claws and scissors.

"Nope," Vi said, hopping up. "See you later."

Tony headed back downstairs as she had hoped he would.

"Don't go anywhere," Vi muttered to the claws.

She strode through the dining room, which was as full of scattered sheet music as the living room was full of science experiments, and past the tiny kitchen.

On each side of the kitchen was a door leading to a bedroom and bath. The set-up was perfect for the two women.

"Jana," she yelled, banging on the door.

Jana responded with a startled shriek.

"It's just me," Vi said reasonably.

"I thought someone was breaking the door down," Jana said, peaking her head out. "Take it easy, slugger."

"Sorry," Vi said, even though the intensity of her knock had been directly proportional to the amount of noise Jana had been making on the other side of the door. "Tony just came up. He said he and Micah are showing a potential tenant around, so we have to pretend to be normal for an hour."

"Good luck with that," Jana replied. But her voice was decidedly playful, so Vi didn't worry. "I guess I can stop singing for that long."

"Cool," Vi said. "See you."

She headed back to her experiment, which she had decided was very quiet and therefore would surely not violate Tony's request.

Besides, this might be the one that finally paid off, and then she wouldn't have to worry about being a tenant anymore.

Violet's grandmother had been, to put it as plainly as possible, stinking rich. And she had left Vi a fortune, but it was locked up in a trust fund, which trickled out living expenses but could not be fully unlocked until Vi opened up and ran a successful small business for one year.

Granny Locke was very fond of small business enterprises. After all, it was her own entrepreneurship that had built the Locke family fortune. And she was even more fond of her hometown of Stargazer, Pennsylvania.

The small town had rebranded itself in the eighties after sending a sort of time-capsule into space with a friendly message inviting any alien tourists in the area to drop by. All of the businesses had adopted space themes, and even the streets had been renamed. After a few decades, the residents had shown no signs of getting tired of it.

And then the big event finally happened.

Vi wondered what her grandmother would think about the fact that after so many years, the aliens had finally answered the call and landed in Stargazer.

She thought that, like herself, Vi's granny would have been interested, but she wouldn't have swooned all over the hunky aliens that now seemed to be on the cover of every magazine and the source of most of the click-bait on the internet. Vi and her grandmother had always shared a certain pragmatic outlook on life.

But unlike her granny, Vi hated the idea of opening a small business. She just wanted to be alone with her experiments. The idea of interacting with the public, day in and day out, was terrifying.

But Granny had set up that trust ten years ago, and the cost of living kept on rising. If Vi wanted to have enough money to live on, and buy supplies for her scientific work, she had to unlock that trust.

Which brought her to her experiment today.

Vi had done the research. Both Baby Boomers and Millennials were more likely to own pets than generations before, after and between. Together, these two generations represented just over forty-four percent of the total US population.

The Boomers no longer had kids in the house, and the Millennials were having fewer children. This meant that the pets belonging to these groups were enjoying a luxurious lifestyle.

Vi planned to cash in on that to build her successful small business. And if she could keep the doors open for at least a year, the Locke fortune would be hers and she could close the business, buy herself some nice lab equipment, and happily shut herself away with her experiments for the rest of her life.

Just the thought of it made her feel pleased. She hummed a little as she applied the first experimental compound to a claw using a tiny paint brush, then reached for her trusty notebook to record the results.

2
___

HANNIBAL

Hannibal strode down the street, taking in the sights of the small town.

Stargazer, Pennsylvania looked a lot like the villages in the movies he had watched to learn about Earth culture. Cars traveled in the center of the street, happy people walked under the canopy of small trees, whose scarlet and golden leaves drifted into colorful piles on the sidewalk.

He gazed into the shop windows. Many of them were exactly what he expected, selling human food and clothing.

But some sold technology that looked unfamiliar to him. Most of his knowledge of the planet had come from the media the people of Earth had sent into space as part of their welcome message. Now that he was finally among them, he was quickly learning how much of their world had changed from the nineteen-eighties version he'd been expecting.

It was all so marvelous.

He was so busy looking in the window of a store that

seemed to sell tiny telephones, that he nearly bumped into a group of women.

"Excuse me, ladies," he said politely.

They all sighed at once, like a herd of zysoons, and smiled at him.

He nodded and jogged ahead, hoping he hadn't blown his cover. Dr. Bhimani had told him it was best to keep his true nature a secret, at least at first.

Hannibal turned onto Crescent Street and scanned the numbers on the houses as they slowly increased, until at last he arrived at the black door marked 221B.

He took a deep breath, ran a hand through his hair, and pressed the button.

A pleasant-sounding chime rang inside, followed by light footsteps, and then the door opened.

Inside stood a small man wearing a purple jacket. At first his face was covered in the grooves that told Hannibal he was an older person. Then he smiled and suddenly looked very young.

"Hello, there," the man said enthusiastically. "I'm Tony. Please come in."

"I am Hannibal," Hannibal responded politely. "Thank you."

He followed the small man back through a wood paneled hallway and into an apartment whose walls were covered in movie posters that seemed to predate Hannibal's limited timeframe of expertise.

Another older man, as large as Tony was small, sat on the sofa, holding a fluffy white dog who let out a low growl at the sight of Hannibal. The man wore a long kimono and the dog wore a matching, jewel-encrusted collar.

"Hannibal, this is my husband, Micah," Tony said, indicating the man on the sofa.

"*Hannibal*," Micah repeated in a rich voice, stretching out the name rapturously. "That's a name you don't hear often enough. Charmed."

He lifted his hand, palm down, to Hannibal.

Hannibal accepted it and shook briskly, just like he'd practiced.

Micah laughed.

"You have a firm grip," Micah said approvingly as the little dog began to bark furiously. "And this is Maybelle. She's just saying hello."

"Hello, Maybelle," Hannibal said to the dog.

Maybelle stopped barking and studied him for a moment, then opened her mouth and panted, her small pink tongue hanging out in a very silly smile.

Hannibal smiled back.

"Well, that settles it," Micah said decidedly.

"No, no, Micah," Tony scolded. "Let's all get to know each other first. Please sit down, Hannibal. Let me fetch us some tea."

Hannibal sat very carefully in the chair Tony had pointed him to. It looked almost skeletal, with its slender wooden frame.

"Don't be shy," Micah chuckled. "If it will hold me, it will hold you."

But Hannibal wasn't so certain. His muscular frame had been designed to be appealing to the people of Earth, but he had already learned that sometimes it meant he was quite a bit larger and stronger than people expected.

He lowered himself down very slowly, hoping to avoid ruining his first impression with this lovely couple.

Sure enough, the chair held him. He smiled in relief.

"You're a big guy, huh?" Micah asked.

"I was designed that way," Hannibal explained as Tony

returned with a tea tray holding three mugs of tea and a plate of delicious looking muffins.

He knew it was okay to talk openly about his true nature with these men. Dr. Bhimani had called ahead to explain the situation.

"Is it true that you used to be a ball of gas?" Tony asked, then held a hand to his mouth. "Oh dear, is that rude to ask?"

"Not at all," Hannibal reassured him. "On Aerie, everyone is a gaseous mass. But when we discovered the message from your planet, our scientists designed and grew human bodies for us in the lab. Then we migrated into them and learned to use them."

"Incredible," Tony said, shaking his head.

"They made us like this in order to maximize our appeal to humans," Hannibal said, looking down at his big body.

"Well, bravo, honey, they nailed it," Micah told him with a sly wink.

That was two winks from these men since he had arrived. Hannibal hoped this meant he had made a good impression and let himself relax a little.

Maybelle stood, stretched on Micah's knees, and then hopped down and headed over to Hannibal.

"Oh, she really likes you," Micah said.

Hannibal offered Maybelle his hand, but instead of shaking it she sniffed it delicately, then hopped onto his lap.

He held perfectly still, hoping not to disturb her.

She lowered her warm weight onto his thighs, curled herself into a tight ball and went promptly to sleep.

"Wow," he said.

"Dr. Bhimani told us she was sending three men to look at the rooms," Tony said. "Where are the other two?"

"Now that people know that there are aliens in

Stargazer, they are very curious about us," Hannibal explained. "Dr. Bhimani has advised us to *lay low*. Together, we draw too much attention."

"Ah, yes, three men like you would draw some eyes," Tony said. "So you'll decide if you like the place, and your brothers will come afterward to check it out, one at a time?"

"No," Hannibal said. "My brothers and I trust each other implicitly. And I'm sure I will like the place."

"It's a lovely apartment," Micah agreed. "It's airy and sunny, with high ceilings - everything you could want."

"However, we have other tenants too," Tony added. "Micah and I live on the first floor, you and the other... brothers would be on the second. And the third floor is occupied by two young women."

Hannibal nodded and tried not to worry about that part.

Dr. Bhimani had warned Hannibal and his brothers that women would fawn over them because of their appearance, and cautioned them not to get involved until they found the woman with whom they would bond forever.

"The women are lovely, but they can be noisy at times," Tony said.

"We don't mind noise," Hannibal said, wondering what kind of noises the women made and why. The woman he'd met so far didn't seem like they made enough noise to make it worth mentioning.

"Would you like to head up and see the place?" Micah asked.

"Yes, please," Hannibal replied.

"Of course," Tony said. "By all means, let's go take a look."

Hannibal wondered how he was supposed to get out of the tiny chair without upsetting the sleeping dog in his lap. He also tried not to be too sad about the uneaten muffins still on the tray. He was a big man with a big appetite, but it would be unseemly for him to snatch up a snack now.

Manners were of the utmost importance on Aerie. He was learning that they were somewhat less important here on Earth, but it was hard to understand which rules were insistences and which were merely suggestions, so he tried not to take chances.

Micah helpfully scooped Maybelle off Hannibal's lap and he eased himself carefully out of the chair. Then they all headed back into the hallway and up the staircase.

Micah was correct, the ceiling height was ideal for Hannibal's large frame. He admired the teardrop shaped window at the landing.

"Victorian charm," Micah said.

Hannibal wasn't one hundred percent sure what that meant, but Micah wasn't waiting for an answer.

Tony pulled a key out of the pocket of his purple jacket and used it on the door off the landing.

It opened into a large living room with windows across the front wall of the building, overlooking the shops. A big sofa was against one wall. The built-in bookshelves around the fireplace held a few paperbacks.

"It's lightly furnished," Tony said in a way that sounded like apologizing.

"It's very nice," Hannibal said honestly.

Tony rewarded him with a warm smile.

They walked into a small dining room and kitchen. Beyond that, there were three doors.

"There are three rooms, one for each of you," Tony explained. "But they're small."

"Each of us will have a room of our own?" Hannibal asked, almost unable to believe they would live such luxury.

"Yes, son," Tony said kindly. "If you like it. This is the smallest."

Hannibal was not Tony's son, but he understood that it could be a term of endearment. He already found both men very endearing. He was glad to think they might feel the same about him.

Tony opened the door to reveal a lovely room with two windows, a bed, and another bookshelf. Wallpaper emblazoned with a pattern of peacock feathers covered the walls and made a sort of circular arrangement on the ceiling.

A funny little curved fireplace, with tiles that had pictures of animals and flowers painted on them, was built into the corner of the room.

"There's another door," Hannibal said.

"It's a closet," Tony told him. "Go on, open it up, look at anything you want. Micah and I will give you some privacy. When you've made your decision, just knock on our door and let us know."

Hannibal was ready to agree immediately. But he was beginning to understand that this was not what was expected.

"I will knock on your door when I decide," he agreed. "Thank you for your hospitality."

"Our pleasure, honey," Micah said.

Tony offered Micah his arm and the two of them headed back through the apartment, leaving Hannibal alone with his thoughts.

He wanted to lie down on the bed and look at the design on the ceiling and think about what it would be like for this to be his home.

But he sensed that it might be improper to lie down on the bed before it was really his, so he went to the window instead.

The living room windows downstairs had showcased a view of the streets in front of the house. But these bedroom windows all looked out over a large garden in the rear.

The area was walled on three sides, with roses growing up over most of the walls. A stone path wound between various colorful plants, leading to a stone bench against the back wall.

It was a very beautiful scene. And Hannibal imagined he might have a good view of the stars at night, there was certainly plenty of sky visible.

He stepped out of the room he already thought of as his, and investigated the other two. They were larger, but didn't seem as cozy to him. The biggest one was in the middle. It had only one window and was painted a stunning royal blue, making it perfect for his brother Spenser. The room on the other side had two windows like Hannibal's, but with three sunny yellow walls and a fourth that was covered floor to ceiling with another built-in bookshelf. Fletcher would love it. Hannibal was sure.

He could not imagine what else he was supposed to be worried about. He hoped that he had taken enough time to have made a thoughtful decision.

He headed back downstairs to find Tony and Micah and let them know that he and his brothers would be honored to take the apartment.

When he reached the landing, he stopped to admire the teardrop window again and heard a door burst open and hit the wall behind him.

He turned to see a young woman struggling with a large box.

"May I help you?" he asked.

She took her eyes off the box to look up at him and he felt as if someone had run a laser beam through his heart.

Mine.

She was small, as almost all humans were compared to Hannibal. And she had untidy brown hair to her shoulders, hastily tucked behind her ears and sticking out slightly on the sides.

But it was her beautiful blue eyes that struck him through. He was very sure she could see right into his soul.

However, she did not seem interested in examining his soul at this time. Instead, her eyes swung over his large body.

Hannibal was used to this. Earth women could not help their appetites.

"Perfect," she said to him.

He felt a flush of pleasure.

"You're big enough to carry a lot," she said, handing him the box.

He took it automatically.

It was surprisingly heavy. As soon as it was in his arms, he was astonished that the tiny woman had been carrying it at all.

"We just need to get this stuff to my car," she added. "Hang on, I'll grab the rest."

He waited obediently.

When she returned, she was carrying an awkward armful of metal poles and cables.

"So you're the new second floor tenant?" she asked. "You made a quick decision."

"How did you know?" he asked her.

Then he felt very silly, because why else would he be in the building? It held only three apartments and he was not Tony or Micah. They were much smaller than Hannibal, and also very old, and they wore very elegant clothes.

"Lucky guess," she said, scowling. "But you have perfect timing. I could really use an extra pair of hands."

He tried to sort out what she had just said. He understood that she wanted him to come with her, and he thought he might just follow her to the ends of the Earth.

But why did she want to have more hands? Was that even possible? It hadn't been listed as an option when they were designing his body.

As far as he knew, humans never came with more than two.

"Sorry," she said. "It's just an expression. I forgot for a minute that you were an alien."

3

VIOLET

The big man's jaw dropped, and Vi recognized her mistake right away. She clearly wasn't supposed to know that he was an alien yet.

She worried that it might even be a little racist for her to remark about it. People were so busy blaming aliens for things around here lately.

It was just that something strange had happened when he looked at her that made her let down her guard for a second. A sizzle of electricity had jolted from her scalp to her toes, and she had forgotten her shoddy manners altogether.

"I'm sorry," she said. "Sometimes I just blurt things out without thinking about it."

"There is no need to apologize," he replied politely. "Did Tony and Micah tell you about me?"

"No," she said. "Well, yes, sort of. They said you were coming and that I shouldn't make a lot of noise while you were looking around."

"I see," he said, one brow raised. "Do you usually make a lot of noise?"

"No," she said. "Jana does, but that's hardly my fault. She's my roommate."

"What kind of noise does she make?" he asked quietly, leaning in, as if he thought Jana was a deranged lunatic, or maybe just some kind of child.

"She's a singer and an actress," Vi told him. "Micah used to be an actor, too. That's how she found out about this place."

"I see," he said, sounding as if he certainly did not see. "And did they tell you I was an alien?"

"No," she admitted. "I could tell by your hands."

"What do you mean?" he asked, looking down at the big hands that were wrapped around her equipment box.

"Most people have callouses, scars, wrinkles, tan lines, something that would give me a clue about who they are and what they do for a living," Vi told him. "But your hands are perfect. They look... unused."

"Wow," he said. "I did not know humans were so observant."

"Most aren't," she admitted. "But I'm interested in details."

He nodded and eyed her with what she could only interpret as respect.

"I am Hannibal," he told her. "I cannot shake your hand because of the large box."

"Violet," she replied. "Nice to meet you."

"Where are we going, Violet?" he asked.

"To the farmer's market," she said. "I'm doing an experiment there. At least *I'm* going to the farmer's market. You're just coming down to my car to help me load this in. Unless you *want* to come to the farmer's market with me. In which case you're more than welcome."

She honestly did not know if she had ever spoken more

words in a row in her entire life. Something about this guy was turning her into a blathering idiot.

"I would be delighted to come with you," he said. "But first I have to tell Tony and Micah that I'm taking the apartment."

"You hadn't decided yet?" she asked, a little horrified that she had hijacked him when he wasn't even her neighbor yet.

"I had decided," he said. "I just hadn't told them."

She nodded and headed carefully down the stairs with her equipment. He followed, his big body sending the whole staircase quivering.

Just like my heart...

Wow. Where had that come from? Vi had never really been the puppy love type.

But she knew the backstory on the guys from Aerie. Scientists had designed them to be like catnip for women. This poor guy probably had every woman he met quivering over him.

Vi thought about what it would be like if she had to walk around knowing that everyone who saw her wanted to touch her, and barely repressed a shudder of revulsion.

"My roommate's car is right out front," she called back to him over her shoulder.

They loaded up and then he jogged back in to talk with Tony and Micah.

Vi leaned against the car door and glanced down the block.

It was a perfect fall day. The air was cool and crisp, just right for sound experiments. And it was awesome that Jana was letting her use the car today. Her only means of transport was her truck, which wasn't the most reliable right now.

"All set," Hannibal said as he stepped outside to join her again.

They hopped in the car and headed down the block to the big municipal parking lot where the market was held every weekend.

"It's like a party," Hannibal said to himself as he gazed at the big banner and the people milling around and eating as live music played on the plaza.

"Yeah, it kind of is," Vi agreed. She had never thought of it that way.

They got out and began unloading.

She'd had the elements for a makeshift booth in Jana's trunk forever, just waiting for a day with the right conditions.

They set it up in no time at the end of a row of other booths. Not bad at all. It almost looked like it belonged there.

There was a moment of panic when it looked like Mayor Smalls and his dog, a goofy but well-behaved Saint Bernard that went by the name of Barker Posey, were headed over to check out the booth. But a group of skateboarding kids flashed past, almost knocking over the mayor in the process and causing him to change course, presumably to give the dangerous delinquents a stern talking-to.

Vi placed a stack of questionnaires, a cup of pens, and a slotted box on the table.

"Okay, ready for step two," she said, heading back to the car.

"Where are we going now?" he asked.

"We have to set up the radio equipment," she told him.

To his credit, he didn't ask any follow-up questions, just followed her back to the car and helped her carry equipment to the little park opposite the lot.

They crossed over a little hillock and Vi looked around.

"Ideally, I'd put it up there," she said, indicating the little knoll. "But I don't really want anyone seeing it. It might skew the results."

"What do we do now?" Hannibal asked.

"We build a radio transmitter," Vi told him.

"Do you need to communicate with someone in space?" he asked.

"Oh," she said. "No, this is a *much* smaller transmitter than the one the scientists used to reach your planet. We just need to reach the farmer's market."

"If we need to send them a message, why don't we just walk over there?" Hannibal asked.

"I'm doing an experiment," Vi said.

"So you're a scientist," he said. "That's fantastic."

Vi flushed. "Yes," she said, feeling pleased.

"Okay, how do I help?" he asked.

They set up the transmitter relatively quickly. Hannibal was so strong and so eager to please that the whole process was actually kind of fun, instead of the sweaty exercise in frustration Vi was used to when she set up her toys by herself.

At last they were finished.

Vi stepped back to admire the device. To anyone else it might look like the skeleton of a gigantic robot hand, but to Vi it looked like exactly what it was, a powerful antenna she had built herself with a capacity far greater than what they needed today.

"Okay, watch this," she said, crouching in the grass to fiddle with the dial.

She had discovered the radio signal for the PA system last week. Now all she had to do was tune to that frequency and play the recording she had for today's experiment.

She made the necessary adjustments, too aware that Hannibal was sitting on the grass beside her, watching intently.

Most times, she would not have wanted anyone hovering, but his proximity didn't irritate her. Hannibal was calm, focused, and quiet.

And there was something about him that made her feel like soda bubbles were being released in her chest.

Focus, Vi, she scolded herself.

She could clearly hear the sounds of a local band making a mockery of a Green Day cover over the PA system.

She took a deep breath in joyful anticipation and made the final adjustment.

The music was replaced instantly with the sound of a sixty-four-year-old opera singer speaking the same word over and over again.

"Why is he saying *Yanny*?" Hannibal asked.

"For the record, he's actually saying *Laurel*," Vi said. "And it was recorded as part of a vocabulary website. But people argue online about whether he's saying *Yanny* or *Laurel* because it's a poor-quality recording, which makes it acoustically ambiguous."

"That is very interesting," Hannibal said, closing his eyes. "Now that you say it, I can also hear *Laurel.*"

Vi nodded. She could also hear both.

"Why are we doing this?" he asked.

"A couple of reasons," Vi said. "First of all, it's interesting. Which is the most important reason to do anything. Secondly, it will help me know the character of the town."

"How would it do that?" Hannibal asked.

But she didn't get a chance to answer because a uniformed police officer was headed their way from the crest of the knoll.

"What's going on here?" the officer demanded. She glared suspiciously at the transmitter as if it had just assassinated John F. Kennedy.

"It's a radio transmitter," Vi replied politely. "And hello to you too, Officer West."

This was far from the first time Vi and Officer West had crossed paths. She was about Vi's age, very clever, and would be considered quite attractive if she ever let her hair down. But Vi thought Officer West had probably only joined the actual police force when she found out Fun Police wasn't a real job.

"You can't do that," the officer responded, ignoring Vi's greeting.

"Why not? It's a free country," Vi pointed out. She knew that wasn't a real argument, but she also knew it was an annoying thing to say.

"You hacked into the PA system," the officer countered.

"Hack is such a nasty word," Vi said thoughtfully. "It's a public frequency. Anyone with a high-powered radio transmitter could easily do the same thing."

"Just turn it off, Miss Locke," Officer West said, waving a familiar piece of paper. "You're in enough trouble already."

Vi bent and turned off the transmitter. "There, are you happy?"

The jangled sounds of the cover band returned across the street.

"Not particularly," she replied. "Would you mind showing me your permit to host a booth at the market?"

"I have no idea what you're talking about," she said.

"There was no *Complaints* booth scheduled for today's farmer's market," Officer West said darkly. "Yet somehow, you thought it would be okay to set up an unmanned booth, without a permit."

"How could you possibly know whose booth it is if it's unmanned?" Vi asked.

Officer West held up the piece of paper that was clutched in her hand and read it slowly out loud.

"Complaint form. Stargazer Farmer's Market. Please check one below. Complaint due to: A - Irritating Yanni sound, B - Irritating Laurel sound, C - Other."

"Other?" Hannibal echoed.

"Some people just like to complain," Vi whispered. "I didn't want to skew the data."

"I'm writing you a citation," the officer said with a sigh.

Hannibal winked conspiratorially at Vi, as if they were planning something. But what? She obviously wasn't going to run from the police over a permit-related ticket.

What happened next was hard for Vi to understand.

One minute the cop was pulling a booklet out of her pocket.

The next her cell phone and radio crackled to life, and a siren began to wail.

"Oh, shit," the officer muttered, patting her various devices and glancing over her shoulder at what Vi had to assume was her police car.

"Listen, Miss Locke, I'm going to let you off with a warning," she told her. "But pack up your stuff and get out of here."

She wandered away, plucking the radio out of her pocket and fishing around for her keys.

Vi turned to Hannibal in awe. "Did you... do that?"

His face froze.

Then he very slowly nodded.

4

—————

HANNIBAL

Hannibal held his breath.

Dr. Bhimani, who ran the Stargazer lab and cared for all the new arrivals from Aerie, had warned them never to show their gifts in front of humans.

At least, not until they had met their mates.

A mate would understand, and not be frightened, or try to exploit the gifts like other humans might.

Hannibal was already certain that Violet was his mate. He'd felt the connection the moment he'd spotted her in the hallway of his new home. The only trouble was that she seemed not to know it yet.

Either way, he could hardly have just stood by and watched her be arrested by the police.

"That's so cool," Vi said at last, smiling up at him. "Was it like, some kind of telepathy or something?"

Hannibal felt his heart stretch as if it were trying to burst from his chest. She was impressed by his gift, and curious, not frightened at all.

"Not really," he explained. "I just have a way with technology. It listens to me."

"That's so rad," Violet said with a smile that told him it was a good thing. "But we'd better get out of here before she figures out how to turn it off."

Instantly, she was on her hands and knees deconstructing the transmitter she had worked so hard to put together.

He helped her as best he could, and then they carried the parts across the street to the car.

"Okay, now just the booth," she said, darting back to the farmer's market.

She moved so quickly. In the movies Hannibal had watched to learn about humans, females were slow and helpless, always falling over a log or losing a heel just as they were about to get away from the bad guy.

Violet did not seem like the type of person who would get hung up on a log, and she didn't even wear high heels.

He felt a surge of pride over his mate's sensibilities, even as he fretted that perhaps she was not gifted at following rules.

They moved between the other booths to get back to hers.

"Hey, Vi," a man called from a booth with several dogs.

A sign over his booth said *Adopt Me.*

Hannibal looked more closely at the man. He appeared to be fully mature. Surely, he did not need someone to adopt him.

Hannibal felt an odd stab of ice in his chest at the way the man was grinning at Violet.

Jealousy.

He knew of it in theory but had never experienced it himself.

He did not like it. Not one bit.

"Come on," Violet called back to him.

He jogged to catch up.

"Who was that?"

"Oh, that's Bill," Violet said. "He volunteers at the pet shelter. He's helping me with my business plan."

"I thought you were a scientist," Hannibal said, trying to keep up.

"Yes, I'm both," she replied. "For now at least."

They were almost back at their booth.

The woman selling some kind of baked goods at the booth next to theirs gave Violet a mean look as they passed.

Hannibal resisted the urge to challenge her to a duel over his mate's honor.

"I have to start a successful small business and run it for a year," Violet said, as she pulled the canvas covering off the pipes that made up the skeleton of the booth.

"What will you do the following year?" Hannibal asked, taking it from her and folding it down as she started taking the poles apart. "Won't you still need your business to be successful?"

Perhaps he didn't understand how businesses worked.

"For the average person, yes," Violet said. "But my grandmother left me enough money to live on for the rest of my life, if I can accomplish this one goal she set for me. So I'm trying to start a business, but first I wanted to do some research to make sure I have the best shot at it."

"According to the New York Times, most small businesses fail within their first year," Hannibal said. Dr. Bhimani often read the paper at the lab. He liked to peruse it when she was done, even though he found many of the articles more confusing than informative. "It is good that you are preparing to meet the challenge."

"Yes, my small business can't fail until the day *after* it has been open for one year," Violet agreed, setting the wooden box, pen cup and questionnaires on the ground and folding up the little table they had been sitting on.

"What is your small business?" he asked.

"Pet manicures," Violet said. "I'm calling it *Pet-i-cures: For the Pampered Pet*. If that name tests well."

Hannibal turned the words over in his head.

"A manicure is for fingernails," he said, uncertain. "And a pedicure is for toenails."

"Yes," Violet said. "But this will be for pet nails. I'm developing a compound that will make them extra shiny. And of course we'll offer organic claw polish in plenty of flashy colors."

"Will dogs enjoy the opportunity to look their best?" he asked, trying to remember why humans painted their nails.

"Probably not," Violet admitted. "But their owners will get a kick out of it."

Hannibal nodded.

"Why not start a business doing something that interests you?" he asked.

"I'm not interested in running a business," Violet said. "I'm just trying to think of a business with low overhead that will make enough money to stay open for a year."

Much about this world confused him. Violet's business idea seemed strange and unproductive, but she seemed so smart. He was sure he would understand her decision in time.

"I will help you in any way I can," he promised.

She paused, her arms full of poles.

"Thank you," she said. "But you have no obligation to help me. We're neighbors - that's all."

"That's not all," he said before he could stop himself.

She blinked at him and her cheeks blushed pink. He was

relieved to see that he wasn't the only one feeling something more between them.

"I do not mean to overstep," he told her. "Perhaps we can speak about it in private?"

"Sure," she replied, looking down at what she was carrying.

Violet had seemed so fearless until now. But at the mention of something between them, she was suddenly shy.

He had seen her response to him, practically felt it.

Surely, she could not deny that she felt drawn to him.

Or perhaps she did not want to be drawn to him.

He tried not to take it personally. Perhaps there was some code of manners that he had overlooked by bringing it up so bluntly.

He decided he would focus on getting to know her for now. Then he could ask his brothers for help when he saw them again.

The men were all equally new to Earth, but together they could sometimes figure out things that they could not have faced individually.

Hannibal helped her load up, and then sat quietly in the passenger seat as she started the car.

Violet seemed very preoccupied with checking the mirrors and adjusting her seatbelt. Perhaps she was hoping not to have to talk with him about what he had said a few minutes ago.

He was eager to put her mind at ease.

"Violet, I hope I am not overstepping what is proper when I tell you that I would like to be your friend," he said carefully.

He could see her shoulders drop an inch as a smile spread across her face, like a rainbow after a hurricane.

"You are not overstepping," she said. "I would love to be your friend."

"Then it is settled," he said, feeling content. "Unless there is some special ritual?"

"How about a high five?" she asked.

He was delighted that he knew what this was, from watching the movies.

He lifted his palm to receive the five, and she smashed hers against it.

A bolt of lightning seemed to shoot through him at her touch, and for a moment he was nearly breathless.

Violet quickly placed her hand back on the steering wheel. Her lips were parted slightly, and she dragged in a deep breath.

So she had felt it too.

This woman was meant to be his mate - he was sure of it, and the bond between them was already strong.

He resisted the urge to roar with delight, and instead tried to watch out the window as the town melted past them.

Don't frighten her, he reminded himself. *Just enjoy her company.*

But he couldn't help stealing glances at her as they headed back toward the place they both called home.

5

VIOLET

Violet headed into 221B with Hannibal on her heels.

She was glad he'd said he wanted to be friends. Vi didn't have the easiest time making friends, mostly because she was more interested in her experiments than she was in sitting around drinking wine and talking about the weather and tv shows.

But Hannibal seemed like he would make an interesting friend. They had already spent a whole morning together, and he hadn't mentioned a single tv show or weather event.

And he seemed into her experiments.

He seemed into her in general. At first, she had actually thought he was going to suggest that he was attracted to her.

The thought gave her a little shiver of pleasure, even as she tamped it down.

Guys aren't interested in me, especially guys who look like that. They like girls who make an effort.

Vi had never been interested in fashion or make-up. She had no desire to fawn all over some man and make him feel smart and strong. And as far as she could tell, that was ninety percent of what flirting was. She wasn't sure what the other ten percent was. Maybe pheromones? Vi made a mental note to design an experiment to test it at some point.

But pheromones or not, Hannibal wasn't interested in her in that way. He wanted to be friends.

Which was just fine. Which was excellent, in fact.

She tried not to think about the jolt of desire she felt when he touched her. There was no point.

When they reached the second-floor landing, she could hear Jana belting out a song about friendship and fidelity. Suddenly, the song made Vi feel a little sentimental. She didn't have that many friends, and Jana was a special one, for sure.

"Is that your roommate?" Hannibal asked politely.

"Yes, she's always singing," Vi said. "Want to come meet her?"

"Of course," Hannibal said.

Vi headed into the apartment.

Jana was standing in the dining room, feet shoulder width apart, singing like she was trying to open some kind of portal with her voice, tears sailing down her cheeks. She did not stop until the song was over, though she could easily see Vi was there with a stranger.

Jana was a consummate professional.

The last note melted into silence.

"Are you okay?" Hannibal asked, setting down the bundle of poles and canvass that had been the complaints booth.

"Yes, yes, yes, of course," Jana laughed. "I'm practicing for a callback, that's all."

"Jana, this is Hannibal," Vi said. "He and his brothers are moving into the apartment downstairs."

"Jana Watson. Pleasure to meet you," Jana said, looking

him up and down in a way that set Vi's teeth on edge even though she never thought of herself as the jealous type.

He's just a friend, she reminded herself.

And it wasn't like it was anything new. Guys were almost always into Jana. She made an effort, but was still perfectly herself. Vi only wished she could sail through life with such unconscious ease.

Jana and Hannibal would make a stunning couple. Jana was unusually tall with a wide, heart-shaped face that she liked to say made her perfect for stage work since she was easy to see even in the cheap seats. Her larger-than-life appearance made his extreme size seem more natural.

If they seemed so natural together, then why was it making Vi feel sick to her stomach to think about it?

"Nice to meet you too," Hannibal said politely, not checking out Jana's dangerous curves.

Vi felt a sense of deep satisfaction, followed by the urge to slap herself.

"I'd like to check in with Tony and Micah," Hannibal said. "They were going to call Dr. Bhimani to see when my brothers would arrive. I don't have a small phone device."

"Sure," Vi said. "Come back when you're done, if you want."

He grinned and headed back for the stairs.

Jana waited until the sound of his footsteps disappeared. Then she arched an eyebrow and gave Vi a significant look.

"What?" Vi asked, rummaging around in the box she had just set down.

"Seriously, Vi?" Jana laughed.

"What?" Vi asked again.

"Vi, he's *cute,*" Jana said. "Well done."

"Oh, I didn't notice," Vi muttered stupidly.

"You notice everything," Jana teased.

"Well, I didn't notice that."

"You should try being more observant," Jana said.

"Ha-ha. Very funny," Vi replied.

"Are you still planning for us to knock on doors tonight?" Jana asked.

"Yeah, why?" Vi asked, grateful for the change of subject.

"My agent called and said they're looking at me for the lead," Jana told her.

"Holy crap, that's amazing," Vi said.

Jana was an incredibly gifted actress and singer, but her large physicality meant she almost always played character roles.

"Yeah, I can't believe it," Jana said. "But it means I have about twice as much dialogue to work on. Is there any chance we can do the polling next week? If not, we can still go out now, I'll just stay up late to work on the script."

"Oh my gosh, please don't worry about it," Vi said, moved that her friend valued helping out with a one-year business plan enough to be willing to delay working on her callback. "I'll be fine on my own."

Jana got a funny look on her face.

"What?" Vi asked.

"Why don't we practice?" Jana suggested. "Let's see what you've got."

"Sure," Vi said. She dashed to her room and grabbed the clipboard she had prepared.

When she got back, Hannibal was there again.

"Vi's just going to practice polling me," Jana said.

"What does that mean?" Hannibal asked, eying the bundle of poles he'd carried in from the car.

Jana got a funny look on her face and Vi realized she hadn't told her roommate that her new friend was an alien.

"It's asking different people the same set of questions to

try to learn information about how people feel on a subject," Vi explained.

"I see," Hannibal said.

"Okay," Jana said. "Hit me with your first question."

"Well, wait, it depends. Can I see your toenails?" Vi asked her.

Jana blinked at her. "Uh, let's say *no*."

"Okay then," Vi said, clearing her throat and referring to her list. "When was the last time you cut your toenails?"

"You can't ask people that," Jana said, sounding scandalized.

How people prioritized nail care seemed like pertinent information to Vi, but she was willing to concede.

She shrugged. "Okay, fine. Um... What is your adjusted gross income?"

"Give me that list," Jana said. "I'll fix it. And you're not going anywhere without me, this is obviously a job for a team."

"You can't come with me, you have a callback," Vi said quickly. "End of discussion."

"I can accompany you, Vi," Hannibal offered.

"No thanks," Vi said.

"*Yes*," Jana said at the same time, giving Hannibal a huge smile. "Give me a couple of minutes to help you with these and you guys can be on your way."

"Perfect," Hannibal said.

Vi sighed.

Jana winked at her over the clipboard.

6

HANNIBAL

Hannibal walked beside Vi through the little town. They had already crossed two streets since leaving their shared home at 221B Crescent Street.

"We'll start at the end of the block and work our way back up," Vi said, indicating the house at the corner.

"Why did your friend want to change the questions?" Hannibal asked.

"If she heard you ask that, she would have both our heads," Violet laughed. "I guess I'm not good at schmoozing people. I'm pretty direct, which I'm told can seem rude."

"What is schmoozing?" Hannibal asked. He liked the way the word felt in his mouth, like melting peach ice cream.

"It means making small talk with people to make them feel at ease," Violet said. "Usually so you can ask them for something you want."

"That sounds strange," Hannibal said.

"That's how I feel," Violet said with a big grin. "But Jana's the people person, and she's right. It's what people are used to. So I have to be careful not to jump right to the point all the time."

"Interesting," Hannibal said as they reached the green front door of the house on the corner.

All the houses on this block were attached, but Hannibal noticed that they each did things to differentiate themselves. The doors were different colors, with various wreaths and decorations. The tiny gardens in front boasted every shade of flower he could imagine.

"Here we go," Violet said.

He watched as she knocked and stepped back.

After a long pause, the door slowly opened to reveal a tiny woman wearing a pair of thick glasses.

"Hello," Vi said, looking at the clipboard. "Are you the owner of Pickles, a mixed breed terrier?"

"Yes," the woman said, looking back and forth between Violet and Hannibal in alarm. "Is he in some kind of trouble?"

"No, ma'am, he is not," Violet said quickly. "We're doing research on pet care in the area, and I have a few questions for licensed dog owners like yourself."

"Oh, no thank you," the woman replied and slammed the door shut.

Hannibal blinked in surprise. "Is that normal?"

"Yes and no," she said. "It's not polite, but it's a pretty typical response when someone thinks you might be selling something."

"But people love to buy things," Hannibal pointed out.

"Yes, but they don't always like to interact with another person when they do," she said. "Which I can definitely get onboard with."

"I thought humans were social creatures," he said.

"They are," she assured him. "But they are also very private."

"Interesting," he said.

They visited a few more homes with roughly the same results.

Hannibal noticed that Violet adjusted her greeting each time. By the third house, the owner was willing to answer some of Violet's questions.

He could see how Jana's wording made the questions more friendly and subtle than the things Violet had initially asked back at the apartment. But Violet was doing a fine job of changing her approach on her own.

They continued on, knocking on more doors, and distributing flyers that announced Vi's soon-to-be business.

By the time they had interviewed half a dozen people, he was getting a feel for the project, and he began to enjoy interacting with the people and their pets.

Violet was clearly feeling more relaxed, too. She smiled more naturally at the people she was speaking with. Hannibal couldn't fathom how anyone could resist that smile.

They finished the first block while the sun was still high in the sky.

The first house at the beginning of the next block had a blue door and matching blue shutters.

He had asked Violet earlier what the shutters were and was amazed to learn that most modern shutters did not actually shut, in spite of their name and their original purpose.

Humans were odd creatures.

Violet knocked on the door and stepped back.

An older woman with short blonde hair and a long flowery skirt came to the door.

"Hello there," Violet said. "Are you Joanne Griffin, the owner of Sassafras the beagle?"

"Oh thank God you're here," the woman cried. "Come in, come in."

Violet exchanged a glance with Hannibal.

But the woman had already disappeared back into the house. There was nothing to do but follow her.

"I must have called sixteen times," the woman said. "Why did it take so long to get someone out here?"

"I'm not sure what you mean," Vi said.

"He was just in the yard, and then he wasn't," the woman said, slumping into a chair.

"Sassafras is missing," Hannibal realized out loud.

"When did he disappear?" Vi asked, crouching beside the woman's chair.

"Two days ago," the woman replied. "It was after dark. He likes to go out for one last jaunt before bedtime. I heard him yapping at something like he always does, and then he just stopped. That's when I heard the engine noise. I ran to the window and I saw a bright light. And when it disappeared... he was gone."

"Is there anyone who would want to take him?" Vi asked. "A business rival or a jealous ex maybe?"

"Do I look like I go around breaking a lot of hearts?" the woman asked.

Hannibal observed her with interest. Her hair was very yellow, that was something Earth men liked. It was said that yellow-haired women had more fun.

Though Joanne Griffin did not look like she was having fun.

"I only meant, is there someone else who would want the dog?" Vi said.

"Mr. Griffin died fourteen years ago, he was the only one

for me," Joanne said with her chin held high. "My Sassafras was taken by those dirty aliens."

Hannibal blinked in surprise.

It was not nice to call someone dirty - he was very certain of that. The woman was probably just forgetting her manners because she was upset about her dog.

However, he could not puzzle out why an alien, or anyone else, would want to steal a dog. From what he understood, thousands of unwanted pets were available for free in shelters all over this planet.

"A lot of people in this town like to blame aliens for everything," Vi said, through a clenched jaw. "But the men from Aerie are here as ambassadors, and there is absolutely no evidence that even one of them has ever hurt a fly."

Hannibal felt a rush of warmth at her defense of his kind. At the same time, he thought back over his own actions since arriving on Earth. He was fairly certain he had never harmed any flies, or any insects at all, for that matter. Which was lucky. He didn't know they were held in such high esteem.

"Ambassadors, eh?" Joanne Griffin let out a cackle. "If that's what you call it, fine. But I hear they're only on this planet to get into women's panties."

Hannibal was even more confused than before. Why would he want to get into women's panties? It seemed to him that they would be much too small to accommodate his larger frame. They would just end up ripping, and then no one would have serviceable undergarments.

But Violet looked even angrier than before. "I assure you, they aren't here to woo your daughter or steal your dog," she said. "Who else would want him?"

"I don't know," the woman said, her tough exterior

suddenly gone, her face crumbling into tears. "He's all I have. Please find him for me."

Hannibal felt his own heart ache at the sight of the poor woman's sadness.

"Mrs. Griffin, I promise that we'll find your dog," Hannibal said, kneeling before her.

"Thank you," she sniffled. "Oh, thank you, Officer…?"

"We're not police," Vi said.

"Y-you're not?" Mrs. Griffin asked through her tears.

"No, we're just walking the neighborhood polling dog owners," Vi said.

"But we will still find your dog," Hannibal added. Obviously, he and Vi were going to help this woman. What choice did they have?

"I should have known you weren't police," Mrs. Griffin said, wiping the tears from her cheeks. "You're too casual, even for undercover officers. But more importantly, you're too willing to listen and to help. The Stargazer force is too busy protecting the aliens at that lab to help the taxpayers."

"Do you have a picture of the dog?" Vi asked.

"What? Oh, of course," Mrs. Griffin said.

She pried herself out of her chair and shuffled over to the fireplace, grabbing a framed photo from the mantel.

"Here he is," she said fondly, handing them a photo.

In the photo a younger Mrs. Griffin held a puppy with long black ears and a small white face.

"How old is he now?" Vi asked.

"Oh he's thirteen," Mrs. Griffin said. "There's a little gray on those ears, but otherwise he's just as handsome. He's full of energy."

"Does he have a microchip?" Vi asked.

"Oh heavens, no," Mrs. Griffin said. "I wasn't going to let them inject some sort of weird technology into my baby."

"We'll look around, Mrs. Griffin," Vi said.

"And when we find him, we'll bring him straight back to you," Hannibal added.

"You're such great kids," Mrs. Griffin said, smiling at him. "Mr. Griffin would have loved you."

Hannibal was not a kid. But he smiled back at her anyway.

"Well, we'd better run," Vi said, grabbing him by the arm.

"Yes, yes, go find him," Mrs. Griffin said. "He has a skin allergy so don't feed him anything, just bring him to me. I'll make him a nice cutlet."

Hannibal allowed himself to be led out of the house and back onto the street.

They waved to Mrs. Griffin and she closed the door.

"What is a cutlet?" he asked Vi.

But she spun on her heel and began to march off toward home.

"Why would you promise to find her dog?" she asked, sounding angry.

"She was very upset," he said. "And she is very old, too old to go looking for her dog alone. But we are young and strong, perfectly suited for such a task."

"What if we can't find him?" Vi asked.

"Surely we can find him. It's a very small town," Hannibal said. "Or so I am told."

"Dogs don't stay within town borders," Vi said. "He could be anywhere. He could be dead."

Hannibal was horrified. That poor lady.

Violet was walking very quickly now.

"Why aren't we stopping at these houses?" Hannibal asked.

"I'm going to go home and post on the community

boards about her dog, since you promised we would find him," Vi said. "Maybe someone has seen him."

Hannibal felt deflated. He had thought he was helping, but he had maybe given false hope to Mrs. Griffin and he had certainly frustrated his mate by taking on a task that might be impossible to fulfill - a task that required her to stop work on her own project.

"How can I help?" he asked her.

"I'll be fine," she said. "I'll see you later."

They reached 221B and she headed inside.

He looked down at the clipboard that was still in his hands and suddenly, he had an idea.

7

HANNIBAL

Two hours later, Hannibal arrived back at his new home.

His heart pounded with excitement at what he had done. Vi would be thrilled to know that the polling on the two blocks was complete.

At first, he had been nervous about talking with strangers by himself, but it turned out that he was good at it. The women especially seemed most eager to answer his questions.

He hoped he had collected ample information to help Vi in her business plan.

And he also hoped that she had made some headway in spreading the word about poor Sassafras.

Hannibal had asked each pet owner to keep an eye out, too. Now that half the neighborhood was looking, he was certain they would find the little dog.

Oddly enough, one of the other dog owners he'd interviewed told him about another missing pet. Hannibal was careful not to make any promises to the sad young man whose pit bull mix was gone, but he did mentally resolve to search for her on his own.

A car pulled up just as he reached the front door to the house.

He watched with delight as his brothers piled out and grabbed boxes from the trunk.

"Hello, Hannibal," Fletcher cried. "It's moving day."

"Come get your box, brother," Spenser said, waving him over from where he stood by the trunk.

Hannibal jogged over, glad to see his brothers.

Earlier that day, they had each very carefully packed a box with their few belongings, in the hopes that the apartment would be a good place for them to live.

Now they each carried their own box up to the second floor.

"I think I know which rooms you will each want," Hannibal told them as he opened the door.

"All of this is for us?" Fletcher asked, looking around.

"Wait until you see the rest," Hannibal said.

He led them through the dining room and kitchen to the three doors that opened into their rooms.

"I was thinking I'd like to take this room," he said, indicating the room on the left. "It's the smallest, but I like it very much. Fletcher, you should take the one on the right, and Spenser, I think you'll like the one in the middle."

He watched as they opened the doors and went to explore their new rooms.

Fletcher threw his box on his bed and ran to the window to look out at the view.

Spenser walked slowly into the royal blue room, nodding his head approvingly. "Yes, brother, this is very much to my liking."

Hannibal grinned and headed to his own room.

His meager possessions would not come close to filling the closet or shelves, but he was glad to have them here. They made this space feel like it was really his.

He wondered if Vi had felt so happy when she moved into her apartment.

"I like my room," Fletcher said, joining Hannibal in his. "Yellow is a happy color."

"It suits your lighthearted disposition, brother," Hannibal said.

Fletcher gave him a friendly shove. "You seem distracted. What happened since we saw you this morning?"

Hannibal did not know where to begin.

"I met the neighbors," he said after a moment.

"Were they unfriendly?" Fletcher asked.

"Oh, they were very friendly," Hannibal said quickly. "One is called Jana - she likes to sing. The other is called Violet - she's a scientist and maybe a business owner. I helped her with a project."

Fletcher's eyes lit up. "Now I know why you are distracted. Women are very distracting."

Women were especially distracting for Fletcher, who was not as uncomfortable with their fawning as Hannibal and Spenser were.

"It's more than that," Hannibal tried to explain. "I think that Violet may be... special."

"Is she your mate, brother?" Fletcher breathed excitedly.

"I don't know," Hannibal admitted. "But I think so."

"What do you think?" Spenser asked, entering the room to join them.

"He thinks one of the neighbors may be his mate," Fletcher said excitedly.

"Is this true, brother?" Spenser asked. "That's wonderful."

"Yes," Hannibal said. "But I've already made her angry. And I don't know if I fixed it or not."

"What happened?" Spenser asked.

Hannibal explained everything that had transpired in his short but eventful relationship with Vi.

"So you completed her task?" Spenser asked.

"Yes," Hannibal told him.

"I think this will make her happy," Fletcher told him. "And perhaps she has had luck finding the dog. That may cheer her up as well."

Hannibal felt much better.

"It is good to have you here, brothers," he told them.

"Today is our moving day," Fletcher said. "When humans move, they have a party with pizza and beer."

"This is accurate," Spenser agreed, nodding sagely.

"Let's order pizza then," Hannibal said. "And maybe Tony and Micah can explain about how to get beer."

"Excellent plan, brother," Fletcher said. "Spenser and I will go introduce ourselves to the landlords, and ask them for their help procuring beer. Maybe they would like to attend our party. Can you call the pizza shop?"

Hannibal smiled. "Of course," he said.

He lifted the receiver of the telephone on the table and placed it to his ear, just like he had practiced with Dr. Bhimani.

He closed his eyes and used his gift, asking the telephone to connect him to a pizza provider.

The handset responded with a melody of beeps, though he had pressed no buttons, followed by a ringing sound.

A bright, happy voice on the other end greeted him and asked if he was interested in hearing about the specials.

"Yes, please," Hannibal said.

"We have one small pizza and one soda for $5.99," the

woman said. "Or two large pepperonis, two two-liters, and two loaded fries for $22.22. And finally, we have our Big Party Special, that one is $85.85 but a bargain for what you get."

"Say no more," Hannibal said, delighted. "I'm ordering pizza for a very special party, so I'm sure the Big Party Special will be perfect."

"Excellent," the woman said.

Hannibal provided their coordinates to facilitate delivery, and was happy to hear that the meal would arrive in thirty minutes or less.

He turned back to his box. He had plenty of time to unpack before the party began.

Twenty-seven minutes later, the doorbell rang.

Hannibal headed for the stairs and Fletcher joined him.

"Spenser is with Tony and Micah, obtaining beer," Fletcher explained. "They said we should bring the food out to the patio in back for our party."

"Excellent," Hannibal said.

It was a nice idea to sit outside to eat, and the patio would give them plenty of space to relax and get to know their landlords.

"Whoa," someone was saying down by the front door. "Are you sure you have the right address?"

"This is 221B, right?" someone replied.

When they reached the bottom of the stairs, Hannibal could see that it was Jana speaking with a person carrying so many pizza boxes that it was only possible to see a hat with a picture of a slice of pizza on it, peeking out over the top of the stack.

"Is this the Big Party Special?" Hannibal asked.

"This is half of it," the guy under the pizza hat said.

"Oh wow, want me to help you carry that?" Jana turned to ask Hannibal.

Her mouth dropped open and she froze.

Hannibal spun around to see what had surprised her.

But the only thing behind him was his brother Fletcher, standing on the bottom step.

He was staring back at Jana, looking equally thunderstruck.

Oh.

Hannibal tried to hide his smile. He grabbed the stack of pizzas from the delivery man.

"I'll carry these outside and come back for the rest," Hannibal told him.

But Fletcher and Jana seemed to have melted out of their shared frozen state. They scrambled to help and a few minutes later, a feast was piled onto the picnic table on the back patio.

"Now I can introduce you," Hannibal said. "Jana, this is my brother, Fletcher. Fletcher, this is Violet's friend, Jana."

"Jana," Fletcher said reverently.

"Hi there," Jana said. "You guys are planning a big event, huh?"

"We planned to invite Tony and Micah to have dinner with us," Hannibal informed her. "But I fear we may have overestimated our nutritional requirements."

The three of them looked at the stack of pizza boxes on the table.

"Would you and Violet please join us?" Fletcher asked. "You can see we have plenty to eat, and we would like to get to know all of our neighbors."

"That sounds great," Jana said. "Violet's up there looking for some lady's dog, but I think she can use a break."

Hannibal felt a stab of guilt.

"I'll run and get her," Jana said. "I'll bet I can dig up a bottle of wine too. Be right back."

She disappeared back into the house and Hannibal watched Fletcher gazing after her, looking like a tortured hero in a romantic film.

Was that how he looked every time Vi left his presence?

It seemed very undignified, yet somehow completely appropriate.

8

VIOLET

Violet refreshed her browser, but nothing had changed.

She had known the chances of finding Sassafras in one afternoon were not good. And she had not even *wanted* to go hunting for the beagle in the first place.

But now that she was working on it, she was having a hard time letting it go. Jana might have used the word obsessed, but Vi liked to think of it as more of a fierce determination to get the job done.

She'd started with a posting on the Stargazer Community digital bulletin board. The dog was most likely still nearby. At its advanced age, it wasn't exactly a big flight risk.

But the board today was more crowded with postings about the Macro Foods corporation scouting the area for a possible housing development. Some people were in favor, some were opposed, and others were in favor but wanted everyone to know that they hated Macro Foods products. An unsurprising number thought the whole thing had something to do with aliens.

This was why Vi never went on the community board.

Jana swore by it for keeping her finger on the pulse of their little town. But if this was the pulse, Vi thought it might be time to issue a do not resuscitate order.

Next, she called the local shelters. She knew the owner had done so already, but she also knew the shelters were staffed with volunteers, and it was likely that calling at a different time might put her in touch with a different person - maybe someone who had seen the dog or gotten a call about it wandering, or just someone who was paying more attention.

She came up empty, again.

Her next move was to try the breed-specific groups. She had posted messages to Beagle Buds, the American Beagle Association, Legal Beagle (a group dedicated to advocating for beagles unjustly accused of biting or destroying property), BeagleMatch (a beagle adoption app) and even The Good Old Dogs, which was an adoption group focused on finding homes for geriatric beagles.

Most of these tiny non-profits had a part-time staff of one, so she didn't expect to get word back quickly.

And now she was going back for another lap around the community digital bulletin board, where her post had gotten buried under an argument about whether or not aliens would be good for the long-term health of the economy.

"Spoiler alert, they will," Vi muttered darkly.

The little town's economy had been bleak until the men from Aerie had appeared. Now the whole town was bustling with tourists hoping to catch a glimpse of one of the hunky heroes.

Just about every woman in the country would climb over their own mother for the chance to spend an hour with one of the guys living in the lab up on the hill. Vi had spent half a day with one, and somehow managed to mess it up by losing her temper.

Good looks and trembly feelings aside, Hannibal seemed like a genuinely nice guy. And it would be very interesting to get to know someone from another planet.

The door swung open and Jana appeared.

"Hey, Vi, guess what?" she said, her eyes sparkling.

"What?" Vi asked, unable to hang onto her own sullenness when her best friend looked so happy.

"We're going to a party," Jana said, waggling her eyebrows.

"What?" Vi asked.

"Okay, fine," Jana said. "We're invited to eat pizza on the patio with Hannibal, Tony and Micah, and...."

"And?" Vi asked.

"And Hannibal has a brother," Jana said, hugging herself a little. "And he's *so cute.*"

Vi rolled her eyes, but couldn't help smiling.

"So come on," Jana said.

"Listen, I didn't leave things in a good place with Hannibal," Vi said. "I doubt he wants to see me."

"He definitely wants to see you," Jana said. "Besides, I'll bet you're hungry, and you honestly wouldn't believe how much food there is down there if I told you. You kind of have to see for yourself."

She was hungry - that much was true. Vi sometimes forgot to take meal breaks when she was really into something, like she currently was with the case of the missing beagle. Not that she was obsessed, of course.

"Fine, I'll come down for pizza," Vi said. "But then I'm coming back up to do some work."

"Of course," Jana said. "Give me one sec to grab a bottle of wine."

"Sure," Vi said.

She headed to her bathroom to freshen up and found herself staring in the mirror afterward.

Her hair was a little wild after the day spent walking around town. She was never one to do much with it other than running a brush through it, which she hurriedly did now, trying not to think about why she was eager to look her best.

Vi had never really worried too much about her looks. She was average height and had the build of a woman who enjoyed a good meal. Her dark hair had plenty of body but little style. She usually just chopped off a few inches when it grew past her shoulders, or when she remembered. Her big blue eyes were her best feature, mainly because they did not require maintenance and therefore could not look disheveled.

Besides, when your best friend was Jana Watson, there was little point making much of an effort anyway. Jana was like a gigantic goddess. She positively radiated style and beauty.

"Are you coming?" the goddess yelled from the kitchen.

"Yep," Vi yelled back, leaving the mirror behind.

When she got to the kitchen, she found Jana with a bottle in each hand. One was a slender vessel of expensive-looking champagne. The other was a jug of cheap table wine.

"I don't know what you have planned, but count me out," Vi teased.

"It's all we had," Jana laughed. "This was my opening night gift from the director of *Pop the Bubbly*," she said lifting up the champagne. Then she glanced down at the jug. "And this is what we can afford to stock our cupboard with."

"Makes sense to me," Vi said. "Oh wait, I have something to bring too."

She rummaged around in the freezer and emerged victorious with two boxes of Girl Scout cookies.

"Nice," Jana said. "Now this party has everything."

They headed out to the back patio.

Vi had always liked the apartment. It was perfect for their needs. But she really loved the little back garden. The vine covered walls made it private, and the beautiful plantings drew in birds and the occasional rabbit. She felt like she was living in a children's book illustration when they hung out on the patio.

And they didn't do it nearly enough. Vi usually had her nose stuck in an experiment, Jana was back and forth to New York, and Tony and Micah had made it *very* clear that the patio was not for experiments, after the tiniest explosion right after she moved in.

They stepped outside into the perfect fall evening.

Tony had turned on the fairy lights that hung from posts surrounding the patio. He and Micah were sitting in lounge chairs, holding hands. Each of them wore a silk kimono in luxuriant colors, clearly in honor of the celebration.

Hannibal and two other gigantic men, unmistakably his brothers, were arranging beer in a cooler of ice.

Vintage Springsteen poured from a small boom box, mingling oddly well with the birdsong from the tree whose branches formed a sort of canopy over the patio.

"Oh, look what Jana's got," Micah cried. "She's my BFF."

Tony roared with laughter.

"Which one makes me your best friend?" she asked, looking down at the bottle and the jug.

"Pro tip, honey. Always start with the good stuff," Micah

laughed. "Then switch over when you can't taste the difference anymore."

"Drinking so much alcohol could be dangerous," Hannibal said suddenly.

There was a moment of silence. Then Micah laughed again.

"Hannibal, my love, I was joking," Micah said. "Of course we will not drink too much alcohol."

"I am sorry, Micah," Hannibal said, looking embarrassed. "I did not mean to insult you. I do not always understand real jokes. They are often more complicated than in the programs we watched to prepare for our journey."

"Like the old woman who couldn't locate the beef," one of his brothers chimed in with a hearty laugh.

"Precisely," Hannibal agreed.

"I'm not even a little bit insulted," Micah said. "You're a sweet boy to think about our safety. But my days of drinking too much are long behind me, don't you worry."

Hannibal smiled and looked relieved.

Vi felt an odd flash of kinship. She was normally the one making the social mistakes. It was nice not to be in the spotlight for a faux pas for once.

"Who wants pizza?" the other brother called out happily.

Everyone cheered and he began passing out slices.

"Hi Violet," he said when he got to her. "I'm Fletcher, and that's my brother Spenser over there."

He pointed to the third alien, who was trying to decide between two cans of soda.

"Hi," Vi said. "It's very nice to meet you."

"And it is very nice to meet you too," Fletcher said. "Hannibal told me so much about you."

She blinked at him, wondering if Hannibal had included the part where she got mad and stomped off like a child.

"All good things," Fletcher whispered with a smile.

She smiled back and he moved on.

Hannibal walked over with four enormous slices of pizza on his plate.

"I wanted to tell you again that I am sorry for earlier," he said. "I did not mean to obligate you in a difficult task."

"It's okay," Vi said immediately. "I'm so sorry I lost my temper. I wasn't thinking. It was really nice of you to want to help. I've got feelers out all over town, hopefully we'll find Sassafras."

"I hope so, too," he said. "I did the rest of the polling. The clipboard is on the table."

She looked at him in wonder. "You did the rest of it?"

"Yes," he said.

"By yourself?"

He nodded.

"The whole block?" she asked.

"I did both blocks," he told her. "I think I got some useful information. And there was another missing dog, but I did *not* offer to find it."

He smiled at her hopefully.

"Wait. There was another missing dog?" she asked.

He nodded.

"That's very interesting," she said.

"It is?"

"One missing dog is just a careless dog owner leaving the gate open. *Two* missing dogs is a pattern."

"Hot sauce, Vi?" Jana said on her way past.

"Yes," Vi said gratefully, taking the little bottle.

"What is that?" Hannibal asked as they joined the others at the picnic table. "It doesn't look hot."

"It's a spicy sauce," Vi said. "I like my food spicy."

"I will try some, too," Hannibal decided.

"Oh, not this stuff," Vi said quickly. "This is ghost pepper sauce. I think we have regular hot sauce up in the apartment. Hang on and I'll grab it for you."

"No, I will try your sauce," Hannibal said, placing his hand over hers and sending a jolt of electricity through her that made her momentarily breathless.

"Oh-okay," Vi said, trying to recover. "Here, I'll put some on mine, then you can do yours."

She dribbled a smaller amount on her pizza than usual and hoped Jana wouldn't rat her out.

Hannibal took the bottle from her and drizzled the same amount on his.

The talk around them had gone completely silent. Tony was up from his seat to watch, and Jana was leaning in.

"Ready?" Vi asked, lifting her slice.

"I was born ready," Hannibal said.

Vi took a bite, enjoying the explosion of heat and smoky flavor.

Hannibal took a bite. He began to chew.

Vi was able to pinpoint the exact instant when he got the kick of heat from the ghost peppers.

First his eyes widened, then his cheeks hollowed slightly as tears began to run out of the corners of his eyes.

He fell to the ground and howled, head in his hands.

"Are you okay?" Vi asked, bending over him.

"I see why you called it *hot*," he said. "My mouth feels like it is on fire."

"Yeah, that's the idea," she said, unable to suppress a giggle.

Fletcher and Spenser were already roaring with laughter.

She watched in wonder as Hannibal reached up to grab his piece of pizza.

"I will finish it, Violet Locke," he wheezed.

"No, no, no, no, no," she said, taking it from him before he could cram it in his mouth. "You win, you did it. No more."

"No?" he asked.

"You ate more of that stuff than I ever could, son," Tony said, coming over to give him a whack on the back.

"I did?" Hannibal asked, looking decidedly more cheerful as he got back to his feet.

"No one on this planet eats that crazy stuff except Vi," Jana assured him.

"That's not true," Vi protested. "There has to be, like, *one* other person, or they wouldn't make the sauce."

"You're the only sane person who eats it," Jana amended. "Well, mostly sane."

Fletcher handed Hannibal a fresh slice of pizza, which he ate with gusto.

"I am sorry, Vi," he said. "But eating spicy things is not something I am good at."

"You're body's still brand new," Vi observed. "You haven't had time to kill your taste buds and build up a tolerance yet."

He nodded in agreement around another mouthful of gooey cheese and dough.

"So what are you good at?" Vi asked.

He swallowed and considered for a moment.

"I can carry an entire radio transmitter and a booth at the same time," he offered with a grin. "Plus I designed an interstellar spacecraft, then piloted it across an entire galaxy to get here."

She was gobsmacked for a moment. He had such an air

of innocence about him, that it was hard to remember that he was actually highly capable of things so complex that no one in her entire species could even imagine them.

And somehow, there wasn't a trace of condescension in the way he mentioned it. It was just something he did. Like taking out the garbage.

"Well, we don't have one of those," she said. "Did you guys do anything fun back at the lab?"

Jana made a throat-cutting motion from the other side of the table.

Oh. Yeah.

Jana had sent Vi an article that detailed how at the lab, the aliens were subject to rigorous, yet humane experiments to test their acclimation to Earth. It also said that their human forms weren't permanent until they found a mate. It was some kind of failsafe to make sure they were good ambassadors. In an attempt to circumvent the process, the aliens were shown pornography daily and encouraged to... take care of business. The government scientists hoped that solitary sexual release would cause them to click permanently into human form without the need for a human mate. From what Vi understood, it never worked that way. The men had to form a pair bond and make love to a life mate for anything to happen.

She certainly wasn't interested in any tales about that part of the experience.

"I mean, um, when you were hanging out with your brothers," Vi added.

"Sometimes after dinner, Dr. Bhimani would put on music," he said. "I grew quite fond of dancing."

"What did you just say?" Vi asked.

"I like to dance," he said, looking confused.

"Vi, no—" Jana began.

"Oh my gosh, There's something you need to try," Violet told him. "I invented this incredible game. I play it when I need to think, but it's a dancing game."

"*Not* the game, Vi," Jana said.

"We have to see the game immediately," Micah chimed in over his glass of champagne.

"A dancing game?" Fletcher asked, looking fascinated.

"Violet, I wish to play this game of yours," Hannibal told her firmly.

"Fantastic," Vi said. "I'll just go grab DancyPants 3. I'll be right back."

"Three?" Micah remarked as Vi headed for the back door.

"The first one didn't work," Jana explained from behind her.

"What about the second one?" Micah asked.

"We don't talk about the second one," Jana said darkly.

Vi didn't even care that her first two attempts had failed, DancyPants 3 was a revelation. She couldn't wait to show it to everyone.

She had just reached the apartment when she heard footsteps on the landing.

"Hey," Jana said. "I came to help you carry it all down."

"You don't think it's a bad idea?" Vi asked.

"Oh, it's definitely a bad idea."

But Jana was grinning so Vi knew she was teasing.

"He *really* likes you," Jana said as they gathered up the components for the game.

Vi almost dropped the amplifier.

"Really?" she asked, turning to Jana.

"Uh, yeah," Jana said. "He almost killed himself eating that hot sauce to impress you. Just try not to set him on fire with the game, okay?"

Vi laughed.

As much as she felt attracted to Hannibal, she hadn't really let herself think about it being mutual. He had asked to be friends, according to *In Vogue* magazine, that was the kiss of death when it came to male interest.

But she found she liked the idea of having a special connection with the hunky alien.

She liked it a lot.

"I'm going to help you get set up, but I need to head out in a little while," Jana said. "I'm staying at Stacy's place in the city since my callback is early. Don't do anything I wouldn't do."

"That's a short list," Vi teased.

"Yeah, but an important one," Jana said.

"What did I ever do to deserve you as a best friend?" Vi wondered out loud.

"I don't know, but it must have been a doozy," Jana laughed.

9

HANNIBAL

annibal gazed at Vi, who was dancing so enthusiastically that her hair flew around her head in a frantic cloud.

If he had thought he liked her before, he was completely besotted now.

He knew they had been dancing for quite a while, but time seemed to have lost all meaning.

The dancing game she invented was truly genius. It had motion sensors that attached to the players' pants, and it awarded them points when they placed their feet in the right spot.

But the fun of the game was making the required foot-work look and feel inspired.

Vi was proud of the data the game collected about kines-thetic response and patterns. But what Hannibal saw when he watched her playing it was her love of beauty, form, and joy.

Watching Vi abandon her interest in the facts to dance like the world was on fire made him feel like he had swallowed a swarm of butterflies.

He looked around to see what the others thought, and that was when he realized they were alone in the darkened garden. The remains of dinner had been cleaned up, and the table was clear.

A solitary raindrop hit his cheek.

"Everyone left," he noticed out loud.

"Yes, they all went in a while ago," Vi said. "But you and I lost track of time. That happens to me a lot when I play this game. Honestly, it happens to me a lot in general."

"I can see why," he told her.

"Well, we should stop because the rain will ruin it," she said sadly, sliding her hair out of her eyes.

"I'll help you carry everything up," he offered.

"Thank you," she said. Her eyes sparkled as they met his.

The rain was falling in earnest now. The cool drops felt good against his heated skin.

He grabbed the amplifier and she took the game and they headed back indoors.

The stairwell felt smaller than before.

Hannibal found himself hyper-aware of Vi's round bottom moving in small circles on the steps ahead of him, the scent of her - clean like soap, mixed with rain.

His heart began to pound as they reached the third-floor landing and she opened the door to her apartment.

It was dark inside, except for the small lamp at the table in the corner.

She turned to him, lips parted slightly. "You can just put this stuff in my room."

It took all he had to restrain his physical response to the idea of joining her in the place where she slept.

The movies he had watched at the lab all began much like this. A man helped a woman with a menial task. She invited him inside. They ripped each other's clothes off and commenced mating or choking each other, or both.

But Hannibal respected Vi. He did not wish to rend her garments. He did not want to hurt her. He wanted to bring their bond to life with gentleness and love.

He nodded, unable to speak, and followed her past the dining room and kitchen and into the room on the left.

Her room was directly over his, then. He smiled, thinking that she would be just above him as he slept.

He had already decided that he would talk with her tonight, that would be all. The idea of a mate bond was something to be ruminated upon, not acted on without fore-thought.

The knowledge that his decision was made eased his mind, even as his body burned to know hers.

Vi's room was cluttered but clean. Stacks of books had been crammed into the shelves at odd angles, an array of surgical tools were laid out on the desk. But the tools gleamed in the moonlight and there was not a hint of dust on the bookshelves.

Her bed was neatly made. The moonlight placed a perfect spotlight on her pillow.

She placed the box of game components on a table in the corner, and he set the amplifier beside them. Then Vi sat on the edge of the bed to remove the sensors from her pants, and Hannibal bent to do the same.

When they were both unleashed from the sensors, he took hers and placed both sets in the box.

He turned back to her.

She was gazing up at him curiously.

His heart sang with sweet agony and he knew the time was now, so he knelt at her feet.

She blinked at him, her ocean-colored eyes wide with surprise.

"There is something between us," he told her, his voice deep with emotion.

"We're... friends," she said a little breathlessly.

"Yes," he assured her. "And we are something else as well."

She waited and he was nearly hypnotized by her beautiful eyes, her plump lips...

"I inhabit this body," he said, forcing himself to focus. "But only temporarily. I can experience some of the joy and sadness of life on this planet. But I cannot fully be a man until I join with a mate. When I claim my mate, I will *click* into this form. And then I can truly know the depth of what it is to be human."

She nodded. She had obviously heard this before.

Most humans had by now. The story of the aliens was salacious, Dr. Bhimani had explained. Humans loved to read about anything to do with sex.

They did not understand.

The mate bond was sexual, but it was everything else as well. It was the elevation of the mate's needs, protection, and pleasure above his own. It was the reason for joy and sorrow, the comfort of family. It was the reason for life itself.

"Violet Locke, I have not walked this planet for long," he said. "But I feel as if I understand everything that is important when I am with you."

"Oh," she said.

"You are beautiful and passionate," he said. "You are creative, and you are honest about your feelings. I feel extraordinarily lucky that you are the human to whom I am bonded."

She gasped.

"Do you feel it too?" he asked her. "Can you feel it when I touch you? The feeling that we are meant to be one?"

He reached out slowly so that she could stop him if she wanted to.

She held perfectly still.

He caressed her cheek, closing his eyes against the pleasure from the surge of love he felt at the gentle contact.

When he opened his eyes, hers were closed. She leaned into his hand, savoring his touch as he had hers.

He couldn't resist stroking her other cheek too, cupping her face in his palms.

She opened her eyes. "I feel it too," she murmured.

He leaned forward and touched his forehead to hers, wishing he could absorb her thoughts and feelings.

She tilted her chin and her lips were millimeters from his. He only needed to close that distance.

Wait until she's ready. Wait until she has thought about it…

But he couldn't help himself.

He kissed her, gently.

She pressed her lips to his more firmly.

He tasted the sweetness of the soda she had been drinking, and the fresh bright taste that must be Vi herself.

Need shot through him and he nearly roared with the effort of restraining himself.

Vi seemed to melt into him, sliding off the bed and onto the floor to kneel against him.

He was drowning in sensation, trying to take in the warm softness of her breasts pressed to his chest, the snug way her arms twined around his neck, and the teasing, delicious taste of her mouth, parting for his tongue.

10

VIOLET

Violet was floating in some sort of paradise.

Surely, she wasn't on the floor of her room making out with a man who looked like he belonged in an underwear commercial or on an Olympic team.

Surely, she wasn't moaning and pressing herself wantonly against him, as confident as a character in a movie, wanting nothing but the next kiss, the next bulge of his muscles against the softness of her own body.

Vi wasn't normally a big fan of people touching her. But this was anything but normal.

She slid her hands down from around his neck, flattening her palms against his pecs, needing to feel more of him to be sure he was real.

Hannibal groaned and slid his hands down to her hips, pulling her more tightly against him, until she could feel how much he wanted her.

She whimpered slightly and he pulled back, gazing into her eyes.

"Are you okay, Violet?" he asked.

She nodded, not trusting herself to speak, afraid waterfalls of nonsense would spring from her mouth.

"We're moving too fast," he told her, his big hand cupping her cheek again.

But when she turned to press her lips to his palm he groaned and pulled her close again.

He cradled her head in his hand and eased them down on the floor, stretching her out beside him, pulling her close.

She moaned against his mouth and clutched his biceps.

He was so strong, his body like a cliff face. But his touch was gentle, loving.

She pressed herself closer, as if she could meld herself to him.

He pulled back slightly to gaze at her, his eyes hazy with lust.

"Violet, I can't make love to you," he said. "Not tonight, not until you decide that this is what you want."

"This is what I want," she said, reaching for him.

"Good," he said with a smile. "I'll just have to hope you still want it tomorrow."

She sat up, panting, frustrated, but secretly maybe just a little bit relieved.

"Let's get you ready for bed," he said, sitting up as well. "It was a long day."

Vi felt weirdly normal going through her bedtime routine with him there. She grabbed her pajamas and ran to the bathroom to brush her teeth and change.

When she got back, he was still there, looking at the wooden labyrinth on her desk. He glanced up at her and smiled.

"I'm not going to be able to sleep," she said.

"Sure you will," he told her. "I'll stay with you if you like."

She nodded.

"I'll go brush my teeth and get changed," he told her.

"It's a sleepover," she laughed.

"No pillow fights," he said solemnly.

"Sometimes I forget that you learned about people from the movies," she said.

"Not anymore," he said softly, observing her.

"Go and come back," she said, feeling suddenly worried about spending even ten minutes without him.

He nodded and headed out.

She looked around her room in wonder.

Everything was the same as before - the same books on the shelf, the same equipment out on her desk, the same curtains with the irises on them.

Why did it all seem just a little brighter?

Could she really be falling in love with an alien?

She thought back to all the guys she'd ever had a crush on.

None of them had liked her back. Vi was too direct. She didn't play games, and she didn't diminish herself to appeal to others.

And when she liked someone, she tended to be even more awkward than usual.

Maybe an alien was what she had needed all along - someone who could take her at face value and judge her on her own merits, instead of comparing her to everyone else.

Footsteps heading back to the bedroom brought her back to the present.

"Did you miss me?" he asked.

He was wearing a white tank top and a pair of loose cotton pajama bottoms that hung low on his hips. Miles of taut muscle were on display for Vi to ogle.

"I did," she realized out loud, trying not to stare.

"I missed you, too," he said, climbing into bed with her.

Vi felt a surge of need at the sight of his muscles flexing and the rich, masculine scent of him.

But he merely curled himself around her, warming her with his big body.

"This feels just right," she said, relaxing into his arms.

"Yes," he agreed through a clenched jaw.

She turned over her shoulder to look at him.

"Maybe too just right," he admitted. "But I'm not sure I can bear to be away from you."

"Tomorrow," she whispered. "I won't change my mind."

"Tomorrow," he murmured into her hair.

And even though she swore she would never fall asleep with him wrapped around her and hormones charging through them both, she found herself yawning and closing her eyes.

11

VIOLET

Vi wiped her hands on her apron and stepped back to admire her work.

The old ice cream truck looked the same as before, but now that the oil was changed and the engine was tuned up, she thought it might finally be ready for the road.

She'd sunk a bit of money and a lot of time into the restoration. But instead of looking at it like an investment, she was looking at her freedom.

Vi's old clunker had died on her a while ago, and she didn't really have the money to buy a reliable car. She had been walking, taking the bus, or borrowing Jana's car ever since.

But then the town council had passed some ordinance to *just say no* to ice cream trucks. Mayor Smalls had led the charge himself, taking a hard line against soft-serve, and managed to get it approved by a narrow margin after months of effort.

It seemed like a lot of trouble to Vi, but apparently ice cream trucks were just too gauche for a town as swanky as Stargazer hoped to be. To her, their jaunty jingles sounded like summertime, but according to a local parents' group, they sounded like childhood obesity.

Whatever the reason, Stargazer's children's loss wound up as Vi's gain. The local dairy sold its ice cream trucks for a song, and she snapped one up right away.

"Vi?" Hannibal's deep voice boomed across the garden.

All her hard work distracting herself this morning was gone in a flash, and just like that, she was practically shivering with lust for him again like some kind of cat in heat.

The whole business was very undignified. It was probably a good thing that Violet Locke had never put much stock in silly things like dignity.

"Back here," she called out weakly.

She had left him a note, letting him know she'd be busy in the parking area for their building, which was on the other side of the stone garden wall.

He surprised her by forgoing the gate entirely and effortlessly jumping the six-foot stone wall instead, landing heavily in the gravel parking area.

"Hello, Vi," he said, his voice low and husky.

She was struck all over again by the size of him. He was well over six feet tall, and positively bristling with muscles. She could tell he had just showered from the droplets still clinging to his dark hair.

She meant to say good morning, but instead she flowed into his arms without really thinking about it.

He bent to press a kiss to the top of her head.

"Talk first," he whispered.

But she could tell by the way he clutched her that he wanted more as much as she did.

She pulled back, trying to make it easier for him. It probably was best to talk first. She had a feeling once the other stuff started happening, they might never leave her bedroom again.

"Thanks for your note," he said, showing her that he still had it in his hand. "What are you working on?"

"Yeah, I didn't want you to think I disappeared," she said. "But I'm a morning person. I was fixing my truck."

"This is yours?" he asked, his eyes widening.

"Yes," she said proudly, giving the cab a possessive thump. "I just bought it last week. I've been working on it. It's finally ready to go for a spin."

"What kind of ice cream do you have?" he asked.

"What?" She realized he was eyeing the pictures on the side of the truck. "It doesn't have ice cream in it anymore."

"We should get some," he advised. "Otherwise people will be disappointed."

"That's true," she said. "Or I can paint it so there aren't pictures of ice cream all over it."

"True," he admitted, looking a little disappointed.

"Hey, are you hungry?" she guessed. Glancing at the sky she could see it was nearly midday. Hannibal had slept late, but of course they had been up pretty late last night.

"Yes," he said decisively.

But then he extended a hand to cup her cheek, his thumb caressing her lips.

Vi gulped.

"Let's go to the diner," she suggested. "I can't cook, and we wanted to talk. It'll be safer there for both reasons."

"Yes, Vi," he said. "Let us go. Do you want to take your ice cream-less truck?"

"We can walk," she suggested.

"That would be nice," he agreed.

"I'll just run in and clean up quickly," she said.

"I'll be waiting," he told her.

She somehow resisted the urge to kiss him and instead opened the gate and headed inside, peeling off her work apron as she went.

Don't overthink things with him, she advised herself, even as her stomach began to twist in knots over the idea of the conversation they were about to have.

Vi had tolerated an obligatory parade of terrible boyfriend types over the years. None had ever lasted long, and she had never been too broken up when things ended.

This was something different though - something she didn't want to screw up. It made the stakes so high she could hardly bear to think about them.

She rushed through a shower fast enough that the water barely got warm, and then dressed hurriedly, not bothering to blow dry her hair.

When she reappeared on the far side of the garden wall, she was happy to find Hannibal right where she had left him.

"That was fast," he said admiringly.

"Um, thanks," she said.

They headed for the alleyway behind the houses. Leaves from the trees in the backyards drifted down, as if in slow motion.

"It's very beautiful, your world," Hannibal said thoughtfully.

"Sometimes," Vi agreed. "Is it very different from yours?"

She knew the answer, she had seen the dry and craggy surface of Aerie in the photographs on the NASA website, just like everyone else. But she thought he might like to talk about it. And she might learn something about him from listening.

"It is very different," he said. "But I was very different there, too."

She nodded.

"The starlight was so bright," he mused. "There was beauty in the contrast between that brilliance and the darkness of the cliffs. But this world..." He looked around, arms extended. "It is lush and soft, much more suited to having a man's form."

He had a man's form alright. Vi tried not to notice it right now. He was revealing himself to her in a more important way.

"It is more suited to you, my mate," he said, pausing to take her hand.

She felt that same pulse of electricity jolting through her whole body.

"Like this place, you are lush and beautiful," he told her, his voice husky. "You are bright and interesting, too."

She was getting lost in his eyes, too hypnotized to thank him for the lavish compliments.

He bent and pressed his lips to hers and she nearly fainted with the rush of pleasure that shot through her.

"Hey you crazy kids," Micah called out from the yard as they passed.

Vi pulled back, embarrassed, but Hannibal kept an arm around her.

"Hi, Micah," she said, feeling the blood rush to her cheeks.

He was smiling at her in obvious delight, as if she had just presented him with a Tony Award. It occurred to her how perfect it was that the lifelong actor had ended up with a real-life Tony as his husband.

Even Maybelle looked pleased, barking happily at the end of her bejeweled leash.

"Where are you headed off to today?" Micah asked.

"We're going to get brunch, Micah," Hannibal said politely. "Would you care to join us?"

"Oh no, honey," Micah said. "Tony's making his special grilled cheese. We'll see you later."

He winked at Vi as she and Hannibal continued past, and she grinned back at him, suddenly feeling glad to share her happiness, instead of feeling awkward.

They reached the side street and then turned onto the main road that led into town.

"I know we are not yet at the restaurant," Hannibal said, "but I wish to begin our talk."

"That sounds great," she replied, squeezing his hand.

He smiled at her, and she thought she would weep at his masculine beauty.

"The mate bond is the beginning of our life together," he told her. "It is unbreakable. Have you thought about what that means?"

"Is it like getting married?" Vi asked.

He frowned.

"I believe it is what marriage is intended to mean. Though I understand that not all marriages are... successful."

Well, he certainly had a point there.

"True," Vi said. "Is every mate bond a success?"

"Yes," he said simply. "The bond is heaven for any being lucky enough to be caught in it."

"Oh," Vi said, a little overcome at the word *heaven*.

A flapping sheet of paper attached to a phone pole caught her attention and snapped her out of her thoughts. On it, was a picture of a shaggy dog with the word *MISSING* and an offer of a reward.

"Is this the other missing dog whose owner you talked to?" she asked, walking over to examine it.

"No," Hannibal said. "That one has very sleek black fur and pointy ears. I think he said it was for herding Germans?"

"A German Shepherd," Vi said, nodding. "So this is a third missing dog. Interesting."

"What are you thinking?" Hannibal asked.

"Three missing dogs is too many to be a coincidence in a small town," Vi said.

"Would someone steal them?" Hannibal asked.

"Sassafras is an elderly dog," Vi said. "And this shaggy one isn't even a purebred. The Shepherd might be worth something, but the breed is pretty common."

They walked on, toward the diner, Vi deep in thought about why so many dogs might be missing.

The jingle of the bells over the diner door brought her back to reality and she realized that she had stopped a conversation about a mate bond with an actual alien in order to look at some silly missing dog poster.

Don't screw this up, Vi, she scolded herself.

But the waitress arrived to seat them before Vi had a chance to apologize.

They headed toward a nice booth by the window.

Vi felt inordinately sad that she would have to let go of Hannibal's hand to sit down.

He surprised her by pulling her in next to him.

"I didn't want to let go of your hand," he whispered to her as they settled in.

"Can I bring you two some coffee to get you started?" the waitress asked.

"Sure," Vi said. "I think I'm ready to order. Do you know what you want, Hannibal?"

"Yes," he said with a smile. "You first."

Vi ordered the special and then Hannibal listed out an

order so long it sounded almost like he was just reciting the menu.

The waitress took it all down with wide eyes and then scurried off.

"You're hungry," Vi said.

"Yes, but food will not sate the hunger I feel most acutely," he replied, gazing down at her.

"Can we hurry this conversation at all?" Vi asked.

"Don't worry, little human," he chuckled. "I will slake your desire. But first we talk, and then we eat."

"Okay," she said, "That's fair."

The words *slake your desire* echoed in her head.

Who talked like that?

It was so cheesy. It was so over the top.

It was so... wonderful.

"What questions do you have about the mate bond?" he asked.

"Have you ever had it with someone else?" she heard herself ask, immediately feeling humiliated at her jealousy.

"The mate bond is unbreakable," he said simply. "I can never have it with anyone else, before or after you, Violet Locke."

"Oh, right," she realized out loud. "What would happen if I said no?"

"I... I do not know," Hannibal said.

"What do you mean you don't know?" Vi asked.

"You are free to do as you wish," he said sadly. "But my side of the bond appears to be... sealed. I have chosen you, Violet. There will never be another for me."

She opened her mouth and closed it again.

That was a lot of pressure.

She knew she should feel trapped, intimidated, afraid, or some combination of those...

But all she felt was relief.

She had met a man - a beautiful, funny, interesting man.

And he was telling her that their relationship was un-screw-up-able.

She had finally found a relationship that was Violet-proof.

"Here ya go," the waitress said, slinging down coffee and platters of eggs and pancakes in front of them.

"Thank you," Hannibal said.

A second waitress joined them, carrying even more of Hannibal's food.

"Wow," Vi said.

"Let me know if you need anything else," the waitress said dubiously.

"Will do," Vi replied.

Hannibal was eyeing her strangely.

"What?" she asked.

"Nothing," he replied quickly. "Let's enjoy our meal."

He began to eat.

She followed suit, surprised at how hungry she actually was. All the excitement must have made her forget to eat much last night, and then she'd been working on the van all morning.

She had finished her eggs and the famous Stargazer pancakes, and was about to reach for her second cup of coffee when her phone buzzed.

She didn't really want to be bothered, but slid it out of her pocket just in case. It was most likely nothing, but when Jana was in New York, Vi worried more than she liked to admit.

But it wasn't a text, the sound she'd heard was the alert that someone had commented on her post about Sassafras on the community board.

"We have a lead," she said in wonder. "Someone spotted Sassafras. We've got to go."

Hannibal dropped his fork and stood.

"Wait, I have to pay the bill," Vi said.

But Hannibal peeled three twenties, a ten and four ones out of his wallet, and rested them on the table.

"Oh my gosh, are you able to read the cash register from here?" Vi asked. "Is that, like, part of your techno gift? Like with the police car?"

"No," he said, smiling. "I took note of what we ordered and added tax and a tip. Came out to seventy-four dollars altogether."

"That's a big meal," Vi said.

"I'm a big man."

No arguments there.

"Okay, come on," Vi said, remembering why they were running out in the first place.

She grabbed a couple of sausage links and wadded them up in a napkin and headed for the doors.

The sunlight outside was a little blinding, but at least they weren't far from home. They could get back to the van in just over four minutes and from there the spot mentioned in the post was about a six-minute drive.

Hannibal jogged along beside her, though his longer legs would have allowed him to sprint far ahead. His expression was serious, and he looked ready to battle a brigade of dog-nappers if that was what it took.

He had her back, no question.

And it felt good.

12

HANNIBAL

Hannibal watched Vi as she drove the misleading truck.

Her mouth was set in a firm line, but her eyes were alive with excitement.

He longed to know what she thought about their bond. It seemed that the day was exploding in front of them with pancakes, missing dogs, old ice cream trucks - anything that could halt the conversation he had begun.

He had opened his heart, told her that his soul was bound to hers, no matter what she decided.

And she had not responded to his unasked question.

The road Vi chose grew more rural as they traveled it. The shops and close together homes of the village quickly melted into more spaced-out dwellings, and then into this area of farmland.

Hannibal knew they were closer to the lab now, closer to the rest of his brothers. He hoped that aliens would not be blamed for whatever had befallen poor Sassafras. Mrs. Griffin already suspected them.

"Here we are," Vi said, pulling the van to the side of the road.

They got out and Hannibal looked around at the fields and barns and a handful of farmhouses. Where they had parked, a paved side street intersected with the main road.

There were no dogs.

"The guy who commented on my post said he'd seen the dog on this side street," Vi said, pointing. "I thought I'd pull over here, so the sound of the truck doesn't spook him."

"Good idea," Hannibal agreed.

They headed off together as Vi fussed with something in her pocket. A moment later, she opened a napkin to reveal several sausage links.

"You were still hungry," he said. "Good thinking to bring a snack."

Hannibal was still hungry himself. He wished he'd thought to bring some food with him.

"It's not for me," Vi laughed. "It's for Sassafras. I'm betting he's hungry if he's been out here on his own. It might convince him to come with us."

"That is very clever," Hannibal said, impressed.

"Not really," Vi replied. But she smiled in a pleased way.

They turned onto the little side street and Hannibal focused on looking for the dog. After only a minute or two, he spotted movement among the recycling bins on the edge of the street.

"Is that Sassafras?" he asked.

The creature did not look like the picture he'd seen at Mrs. Griffin's house. That one had been a baby. This one looked older and more jaded. Mrs. Griffin had told them that he was a beagle, like the famous Snoopy from the Halloween program.

Hannibal didn't see the resemblance.

"That's him," Vi said excitedly. "Just follow my lead."

She moved slowly and calmly, easing closer to the dog.

When it finally noticed her, she held out the sausages.

"Hey, Sassafras," she sang in a low, soft voice. "Hey, buddy. Do you want some sausages? Come."

The dog turned to her and jogged forward, its chain collar clinking merrily.

"Hi," Vi said, sitting on the ground and letting the little dog climb all over her.

First, he sniffed her face. Then he washed it thoroughly with his tongue.

Then, and only then, did Sassafras accept the sausages, which he downed enthusiastically in as few bites as he could, without saving any for anyone else.

"Mrs. Griffin is going to be so happy," Vi said, turning to Hannibal.

"Yes," he agreed, happy that they had found the missing pet and even more happy that Vi was happy.

"How did you get out here?" Vi asked the dog.

But he merely panted at her and licked her nose again.

"Want to hold him while I drive?" Vi asked.

"Yes," Hannibal said immediately. He very much wanted to know what the fuzzy creature felt like. There had been no pets in the lab. And he hadn't been able to enjoy holding Maybelle on his lap, because he'd been worried about making a good impression.

He admired the little dog's positive attitude in spite of compromised circumstances.

"Here, take him," Vi offered.

Hannibal bent and put his arms out.

The little creature waddled to him immediately.

Hannibal cradled the dog to his chest, reveling in the feeling of contentment that instantly filled him.

The dog's wet tongue caressed Hannibal's nose and he threw his head back and laughed.

"Dogs are the best, right?" Vi asked.

"I think you're right," Hannibal told her earnestly.

"Well, let's get him back to his mom," Vi said, heading for the truck.

"I think Mrs. Griffin would like to see him first," Hannibal suggested.

"What—oh," Vi said. "Yes, you're right that's weird, isn't it? When we adopt pets, we tend to think of them like our children. Mrs. Griffin is the mom I meant."

"Oh," Hannibal said, looking down at the ball of fluff in his arms.

He did have feelings for it already. And it was not even his companion creature. The dog was the property of Mrs. Griffin. It seemed odd that one creature on this planet could claim ownership over another, but the dogs seemed to enjoy it, so Hannibal figured it must be okay.

They got back to the van and he climbed in carefully, securing his seatbelt in such a way as not to interfere with the little dog.

"Mrs. Griffin is going to be so glad to see him," Vi said.

Hannibal loved the look of happy anticipation on his mate's lovely face. The tension she sometimes wore on her exterior was gone, replaced by joy. And it was because she was going to make someone else happy.

Yesterday, he had been concerned that Vi might be more interested in experiments than she was in connecting with other beings.

But now he could see that her businesslike front hid the kind of warm-hearted motivations and desires that made him proud to be her mate.

If she would have him...

For a moment he allowed himself to think about what would happen if she refused.

His blood seemed to freeze in his veins. He felt his lungs forget to fill with air, and his heart began to pound frantically.

Sassafras licked his nose again, as if realizing his condition.

Hannibal took a deep breath and willed his heartbeat to slow.

"You okay?" Vi asked.

"Yes," he said. "Of course. I am fine, Vi."

"Good, because we're here," she said.

They got out and headed up to the house on the corner with the blue shutters. Vi knocked and Hannibal could hear footsteps head toward the door from inside.

The door opened and there was an immediate scream.

"*Sassafras,*" Mrs. Griffin shrieked with joy, reaching for the little creature. "Who's my sassy boy?"

Hannibal surrendered the dog at once and turned to Vi.

She was smiling as she watched Mrs. Griffin press kisses on the furry little head.

"Come in, come in," Mrs. Griffin said, disappearing inside.

They followed her into the house. She headed past the living room where they had visited with her before and into a small kitchen.

"I have to put you down, Mr. Sass, so I can fix your food," she crooned. "Be a good boy."

She placed the dog on the floor and rummaged in the cupboard, pulling out a can.

"I'm so grateful," she enthused as she opened it and grabbed a bowl. "I can't really afford to pay a reward, though."

"No need," Vi said at once. "That's not why we helped you."

Mrs. Griffin turned with the bowl of dog food and then gasped.

Sassafras was sitting politely, smiling up at her with his tongue hanging out.

"What's wrong?" Hannibal asked.

"He's acting weird," Mrs. Griffin said. "He doesn't normally do that."

"Do what?" Vi asked.

"Stare," Mrs. Griffin said. "He usually jumps on me and barks when I'm fixing his dinner."

"Maybe he's tired," Vi suggested.

"Maybe," Mrs. Griffin said.

She placed the bowl on the floor.

Sassafras smiled up at her expectantly, wagging his tail.

"Why isn't he eating?" Mrs. Griffin said worriedly.

"I did lure him over to me with some sausages," Vi admitted.

"That wouldn't stop him," Mrs. Griffin said. "Nothing ruins his dinner. Eat, Sassy, eat."

She tapped the side of the bowl and the little dog sprang into action, wolfing down the food like he thought she was going to take it away. He had clearly just been waiting to be told it was okay to eat. Hannibal could definitely sympathize with that.

"That's strange," Mrs. Griffin said.

They watched as Sassafras gulped down the last of his food.

When he was finished, he sat down and smiled up at them, as if to ask what they were planning to do next.

"He's really acting funny," Mrs. Griffin said. "He's quiet. Too quiet."

Vi nodded, her lips pressed together.

"Where did you find him?" Mrs. Griffin asked.

"At the intersection with Lindbergh Lane," Vi said. "He was sniffing some recycling containers."

"Well, I'm glad you brought him back, but I don't love that you put a choke chain on him," Mrs. Griffin sniffed. "That was unnecessary. I'm sure he would have come with you willingly."

"We didn't put that collar on him," Vi said.

"You didn't?" Mrs. Griffin asked.

"No, of course not," Vi said. "I thought that was his regular collar."

"Oh, Sassy, what happened to you?" Mrs. Griffin wailed, lowering herself to the floor beside her panting dog. "That thing is around your neck and you're so *quiet*. What did you *see?*"

Hannibal wondered what a dog would have to see to make him not bark.

He suspected the animal might be subdued merely because he was tired and had been on some sort of adventure, but Mrs. Griffin appeared convinced that the dog had been violated in some way.

"Does he have a favorite toy?" Vi asked. "Maybe we can play with him and he'll get his energy back."

"Oh, that's a good idea," Mrs. Griffin said. "Help me up."

Hannibal took her hands and helped her to her feet.

"Let's go get your dolphin," Mrs. Griffin said to Sassafras in an animated voice.

Sassafras followed after her, a delighted expression on his canine face.

Mrs. Griffin grabbed a blue rubber dolphin toy from a basket in the living room and squeezed it.

A high-pitched squeak issued from it.

Sassafras sat and wagged his tail.

"He should be barking," Mrs. Griffin said worriedly. She threw the toy.

Sassafras's tail wagged faster, but he didn't move.

"What are you doing? Go get it," Mrs. Griffin begged.

The dog flew after the toy, grabbed it in his mouth, and galloped back to her with it so fast his ears blew backward.

He dropped it at her feet and then sat, smiling proudly and wagging his tail.

"This isn't my dog," Mrs. Griffin said firmly.

"What?" Vi asked.

"They replaced him," Mrs. Griffin said.

"But he matches your description," Vi said. "He's the right age, in the right town. He obviously knows you. There's a picture of him right over there."

Mrs. Griffin shook her head. "Something's not right."

Sassafras whined up at Mrs. Griffin, who had begun to sob.

Hannibal sat on the floor, offering comfort to the poor creature.

"I'm sure this is your dog, Mrs. Griffin," Vi was saying. "He's probably just a little traumatized from being away from you. We'll figure out what happened to him. Just give him a little time to adjust to be home."

"Hello, Sassafras," Hannibal said quietly. "Your human mother is upset because she missed you. See if you can remember how to behave in your normal manner."

Sassafras merely gazed back at him with sad eyes. Hannibal wondered if the human who created Snoopy had ever actually seen a real beagle.

"Grab that collar," Vi advised Hannibal. "We'll check it out."

"Are you going to find my real dog?" Mrs. Griffin asked hopefully.

"We're going to see if we can find out what happened," Vi said. "But you need to keep this dog and take care of him. Can you do that for us?"

Mrs. Griffin looked suspiciously at the dog.

The dog smiled up at her, wagging his little tail.

"Of course," she said sadly. "I never could resist a beagle."

Hannibal slipped the chain off the little dog's neck and handed it to Vi, who looked it over briefly and nodded.

"Okay for us to take this?" she asked Mrs. Griffin.

"I never use those brutal things," Mrs. Griffin sniffed. "You can throw it out for all I care."

Vi headed back to the truck with a look of concentration on her face, and Hannibal followed.

13

VIOLET

Vi got back in the truck and pulled away from the house, her thoughts racing.

"Where are we going?" Hannibal asked, reminding her that she wasn't alone.

"The pet shop," Vi replied. "Where we can get a lead on this."

"How do you know?" Hannibal asked.

"The chain collar," Vi said. "It's practically brand new."

She tossed it to him and pulled out of the parking space.

"It's metal," he said. "How can you determine its age?"

"See how shiny it is?" Vi asked. "Do you see any nicks or imperfections?"

"Well, no," Hannibal said.

"Dogs aren't careful with these things," Vi explained. "They squeeze under things, scratch at themselves, and smash into walls and furniture when they're playing. That choke chain is light blue. Even though it looks metallic the blue color is really a sealant. If he had been wearing it for long it would already be nicked and flaking away in spots. Do you see any nicks?"

"Only one or two," Hannibal said, examining it more closely.

"So it's new," Vi said.

"Is there only one pet shop nearby?" he asked.

"There are three within easy driving distance," Vi said. "But I'm willing to bet this came from the local shop right in Stargazer. Look at the stamp on the tag."

"TrainPro," Hannibal read.

"Exactly," Vi said. "That's the brand of gentle leader leash that Micah and Tony use for Maybelle. Tony said the local shop is the only place that carries that brand, so he got it there in spite of the price. I'm guessing that whoever put that collar on the dog bought it there."

"Amazing," Hannibal said.

"It's only amazing if I'm right," Vi said, trying to concentrate on the road instead of basking in the fact that Hannibal was enjoying her skills.

She parked right out front and then cursed quietly.

"What's wrong?" Hannibal asked.

"I don't have change for the meter and I *always* get a ticket," Vi said.

"Hm," Hannibal said, hopping out of the car and looking at the meter.

She watched him blink at it.

Then he waved her out.

By the time she joined him he was wedging a one-dollar bill in the slot.

"I don't think it works that way," she told him.

"Oh no, I fixed it so that it's showing a dollar of credit," he said. "But I wouldn't like to steal."

She smiled up at him in amazement, choosing not to tell him that the next person to walk past would probably swipe the dollar. It was his intention to do the right thing that was important. It meant everything to her.

"Everything okay?" he asked her.

"Y-yes," she managed. "Everything is great."

He smiled and it took everything she had not to go up on her toes and kiss him.

But there was a mystery to be solved, and somehow, she had managed to stop them from having their conversation earlier.

She wondered bleakly if she could manage to wrap up this dog thing in time for them to have a minimal talk before she tackled him into bed.

Hopefully, he would take her word for it that she knew what he was asking, and they could just get down to business.

She turned on her heel and headed into the pet shop, desperate to get her mind off Hannibal's imposing body.

The shop was bright and cheerful inside. Someone had painted a mural of pets in space ships along the left wall.

The owner was busy talking with a woman by the lizard cages.

Vi headed to the community bulletin board.

The shaggy dog's poster was up along with one for a German Shepherd and two others.

"Damn," she murmured.

"That's a lot of missing dogs," Hannibal said.

She looked back to the owner of the shop, but he was still talking to the lizard lady. They seemed to be discussing enclosures. They would probably be at it for a while. Enclosures were the jumping off point - they still needed to talk food, heat lamps, substrate, and decor.

"Let's see if we can find the chain collars," she said.

Hannibal nodded.

They headed down an aisle past endless permutations of tennis balls attached to pieces of colorful rope. A woman with a Great Dane on a leash was comparing two options which Vi knew would look exactly the same color to the more limited photoreceptors in a dog's eye. She decided it was better not to inform the woman of that fact.

On the aisle cap, a man was trying a t-shirt that said *My Other Human is Han Solo* on a very patient bull dog mix.

The next aisle had jars of treats and training items. A woman with two small dogs on matching leashes searched the rack of books as the dogs jumped, whined, and got tangled around her and each other.

Hannibal bent to look at something.

Vi waited but didn't notice what he was looking at.

She had caught sight of the collars in the next aisle.

A man stood in front of them, studying them carefully and fingering the materials.

He already had at least a dozen collars in his arms.

How many dogs does he have? Vi thought to herself.

But she didn't get a chance to expand on the thought because dogs all over the store began barking and howling.

The two in the aisle with the woman looking at training books were closest to Vi and the sound was overwhelming.

She wanted to curl up in a ball until it was over, but instead she took three deep, calming breaths and then turned to check on Hannibal.

He was holding a training whistle, and blowing on it with all his might. That was what had caught his eye. She cursed herself for not sticking around long enough to stop him.

"I think it's broken," he said, holding it out to Vi. "I can barely hear it."

He moved as if to put it in his mouth again and she snatched it.

"That's a dog whistle," she explained. "You shouldn't be able to hear it at all. The pitch is above what human ears can hear. But it's audible to dogs, that's why they're all crying. The pitch is high enough to irritate them."

"I did not know there were frequencies humans could not hear," Hannibal said, looking confused.

"Oh yes," Vi told him. "We can hear only a small range of the sound spectrum. As a matter of fact, as we age, our hearing deteriorates, so there are some sounds that can be heard only by younger people. Jana uses something like that for her ringtone, so she won't disturb Tony and Micah. I bet you can hear the whistle because technically, your ears are brand new."

A whole world of audio experiments unfolded before her. She pushed the thoughts aside for another time.

"I see," Hannibal said. "I'm very sorry I disturbed the dogs."

"They'll be fine," Vi said, smiling reassuringly at him.

Already, the dogs seemed to have forgotten.

Vi looked around, trying to remember what she had been thinking about before the whole store exploded in barking.

The collars...

She headed for the collar aisle, but it was too late, the man was already gone.

She jogged for the cashier's station.

"Vi, where are you going?" Hannibal called out.

She heard his footsteps behind her, but she didn't slow down.

She was pinning all her hopes to the lizard lady now. If

she was still here asking questions or checking out, there was no way collar man could have gotten anywhere.

But when she reached the cash register the owner was standing there alone.

"Hi there, how can I help you?" he asked.

"What happened to the lizard lady?" Vi practically whined.

"What?" the man asked.

"The lady who was looking at lizards," Vi said, recovering. "I just thought she was going to buy one, she seemed really interested."

"Nah," the man said, shrugging. "She was just looking."

"Oh," Vi said, wondering how she could possibly segue into asking him about the collar guy.

"So what can I do for you?" the man asked.

Hannibal had joined Vi and was standing next to her now.

"We'd like to buy, um..." Vi racked her brains.

"This," Hannibal said, handing over the whistle.

Vi managed not to audibly sigh in relief.

"Testing it out earlier, weren't you?" the man chuckled, ringing them up.

"There sure are a lot of missing dogs up on your board," Vi said. "Are those posters all current?"

"I take them down every week," the owner said sadly. "There are just a lot of missing dogs the last few days."

"There was a guy here just a minute ago, looking at collars," Vi said.

"Oh, you mean Phil Jessing?" the owner asked.

"I guess," Vi said. "Looked like he had about a dozen collars. Do you think he might have anything to do with so many missing dogs?"

"Who, Phil?" the owner asked, chuckling. "Nah, not him."

"He just has a lot of pets?" Vi asked.

"You could say so," the owner laughed.

Vi had no idea why the owner was laughing, but could only assume it meant the guy was one more pet-obsessed regular.

"Where does he live?" Vi asked, hoping he might share the info even though it probably was a privacy violation.

"You kids want to go see Phil, eh?" the owner looked them up and down with interest. "I think he'd be just fine with that. He's out on Lindbergh Lane. Just wait until after dark, and then knock on the double doors at the big red barn."

Vi spun to face Hannibal.

Lindbergh Lane was where they had found Sassafras.

"Thanks," she said as they paid for their purchase and headed out.

14

HANNIBAL

Hannibal stood beside Violet as they both gazed at the double doors of the red barn.

The sun was down now, and the other stars seemed hardly visible on this planet. He could just make out Vi's face glancing nervously up at his and the gleam of moonlight on her dark hair.

"Ready?" she asked.

"Whenever you are," he replied.

He was more than ready, after spending the afternoon cooling his heels and helping Vi do some more work on her truck.

They had driven by earlier to do what Vi referred to as reconnaissance, but there was no sign of anyone, man or dog, anywhere in the vicinity. They had briefly considered breaking into the barn, but decided that might be taking things a bit too far.

The man at the pet store had told them to wait until after dark before seeking out Mr. Phil Jessing, and so that was exactly what they did.

Vi extended her hand and knocked on the heavy door.

On the way over, they had discussed what they might find. Vi wasn't sure why anyone would want to kidnap such an array of different dogs, but she feared there might be experiments going on, or worse.

If that was the case, they needed to be prepared to act. She had even brought up the contact for the local police on her tiny phone, just in case she needed to dial it in haste while Hannibal created a distraction.

He had asked why she didn't call the police to begin with. But she had reminded him that the police didn't exactly see eye to eye with her because of some of her experiments, and that she doubted they would come out without cause on her behalf.

The barn door began to slide open on its track.

Inside was as dark as outside, except for candles placed at intervals around the space.

It occurred to Hannibal that barns were susceptible to fire, and that candles might not be the best idea. Especially if there were enthusiastic dogs about.

Then he ceased to notice anything about the candles.

A man appeared at the door wearing nothing but a pair of very small leather underpants and a black leather collar. His skin was damp and looked almost oily in the candlelight.

The man ran a hand through his blond hair as he looked Vi and Hannibal up and down.

"Heyyyyy," he said in a low, pleased voice. "Come in."

Vi looked almost frozen, but she allowed the man to lead her inside.

Hannibal followed.

"Hey guys," the man called out. "We've got some newbies tonight. Are you guys from around here?" he asked, turning back to Vi and Hannibal.

"Yes," Hannibal disclosed.

Vi was just opening and closing her mouth like a fish.

Other people stepped out of the shadows around the big barn. Many of them were dressed much like the man who had let them in. But some were dressed more like Hannibal was used to.

"Let me guess," the man said. "She's the dom."

"Excuse me?" Hannibal asked.

"She is the dominant one in your relationship, right?" the man asked, waggling his eyebrows.

"She makes the decisions," Hannibal agreed. Then he waggled his eyebrows too, to be polite.

He looked around again, but he didn't see any dogs.

"Show us what you've got," the man said, gesturing to a corner of the barn near one of the candles.

Hannibal headed over obediently.

"Wait, wait," the man said. "You gotta at least take your shirt off. The rest of us are in full gear."

Very little of what the man was saying made sense to Hannibal. But *take your shirt off* was something he understood, and it was easy enough to do.

While the gathering watched, Hannibal peeled off his t-shirt.

There were murmurs of approval and awe.

Hannibal smiled. He was glad if they were amused, but it was Vi he wanted to impress.

He glanced down at her and found she was staring openly at him.

A shiver of hot desire electrified him, and he momentarily forgot himself and bent to kiss her.

"No," Vi said firmly.

He stood up straight, feeling as if he had been slapped.

"Ohhh, you know what you're doing," their host murmured. "Go on, take your place."

"Come," Vi said, heading toward the corner.

Hannibal followed, feeling like a scolded puppy.

"Just go along with this," Vi whispered. "It's a BDSM club. We'll find a way out in a minute or two, but we can't embarrass them by telling them we're not into it. We might still get a lead out of this."

Hannibal racked his brain for anything those letters could stand for, but came up blank. He looked around one more time, then remembered a scene from one of the videos he'd been shown back at the lab. Everything clicked into place.

"I don't think those collars were for dogs," Hannibal whispered back.

"Correct," Vi said. "This was a... miscalculation on our part. But it was still our best play, since we found Sassafras out here."

"Okay, people, keep oiling up," the host yelled out. "We'll start the activities in a few minutes."

"My God," Vi whispered.

She was looking at a small dish filled with a clear liquid.

"Sorry, Hannibal," she whispered and plunged her hands into the dish, pulling them out covered in glistening liquid of some kind. "Hold still. And no matter what happens, don't touch me."

He planted his feet shoulder width apart, ready to do whatever she wanted.

When she placed her hands on his bare shoulders, the pleasure started moving through him in waves.

The liquid was warm and slick, and it made the movement of her skin against his feel silky and smooth.

Vi slid her hands down his chest, moaning lightly, though he wasn't sure she knew she was entirely aware of it.

Her hungry sound set off a storm of lust inside him and he clenched his fists to stop himself from grabbing her as her hands slid over his ribcage and explored his abs.

He was reeling with need, his cock so hard it hurt.

All around them, the other couples were oiling up, too. The sight did nothing for him. He turned his head to evade it.

He wanted only Vi and the warm agony of her teasing hands sliding over every inch of him.

He bit back a groan as she moved away from him to dip her hands in the oil once more.

"You should be just about finished up and ready to swap now," the host called out.

Swap?

Vi's eyes had gone wide.

Suddenly she fell to the floor, the dish landing beside her with a loud clatter.

"Oh my gosh, what happened?" the host asked, rushing over.

Vi opened her eyes and winked at Hannibal, then closed them again.

She was pretending to be ill.

She was very, very smart, Hannibal realized with a sigh of relief.

"I think she fainted," Hannibal said, scooping her up in his arms. "She was very nervous about tonight. I'd better get her home."

"That happens," the host said sadly. "Be sure to come back next month."

"We will remember," Hannibal said, feeling bad about

the implied affirmative, but wanting desperately to get out before anyone else tried to put oil on him.

He strode out the barn doors and carried Vi all the way to the van.

When he reached the far side of it, where he was sure he couldn't be seen from the barn doors, he paused.

"Vi, are you okay?" he asked.

"Yeah," she whispered back. "That was a close one."

He placed her gently on the ground.

She was panting slightly, and though her eyes were fixed on his, he knew to his soul that she was still imagining sliding her hands up and down his body.

"We must go home," he told her, and himself, firmly. "We must have privacy and time."

But her eyes were hazy with lust and he bent to kiss her just once.

Suddenly her phone made a loud noise.

She blinked, shook her head as if to clear it, and pulled her phone out of her pocket.

"Jana's home," she said, then climbed into the driver's seat.

So much for privacy.

15

VIOLET

Vi drove in silence, trying not to think about the big hunky alien beside her, using his shirt to wipe away the remaining oil from his muscular chest.

Tonight had been awkward, but unbelievably sexy.

Unfortunately, the text that interrupted them a moment ago was from Jana, who was home from New York and excited to talk with Vi about her audition.

Which meant their private apartment was now occupied again. And while Jana had brought home guys before, Vi had not. And she had a feeling that what she was planning to do with Hannibal tonight might get noisy.

She suppressed a shiver of desire and tried again to focus on the road and the physical act of driving the truck.

It was surprisingly easy to drive. In spite of its size, it had a good turning radius and the brakes were sensitive.

She tried to envision driving this thing around Stargazer for the next year or so, trimming dog nails.

It wouldn't be that bad if Hannibal was there to help.

It wouldn't be that good, either, but it was only a year.

Overall, things were looking up in a big way for Vi.

She had a best friend and an alien boyfriend, and a temporary career of sorts picked out.

She pulled up behind 221B with a smile on her face, and they headed through the gate. The garden was silent and beautiful in the moonlight.

When they reached the entry hall, Vi noticed there was mail in her basket. She fished it out.

"What's that?" Hannibal asked.

"Just a piece of mail," she replied. "That basket is for your apartment."

His was empty. Aliens probably didn't have a lot of pen pals.

She gazed down at the envelope and her heart leapt.

The return address was *M. Croft*, which meant it was from the trust. Based on the thinness of the envelope, it was probably just confirming that they had logged her business idea and would await her next message alerting them that the business was open, so that her one-year timer would start.

She tore open the envelope and quickly scanned the letter.

Her heart dropped.

Tears burned in her eyes, and it was hard to read it again, but she did so, and one phrase seared into her mind.

...regret to inform you that we are rejecting your proposal for a mobile pet grooming business, as it is not considered a seemly enterprise...

"Not a seemly enterprise," she hissed. "Grandma's enterprise wasn't exactly highbrow either."

"Vi, what's wrong?" Hannibal asked.

"Nothing," she said, folding the letter and wadding it into her pocket. "I just got some bad news about my business idea."

"I'm so sorry," he said, opening his arms to her.

But suddenly she didn't want to be close with him. She didn't want to be close to anyone.

Vi was feeling awful. She had always needed her space, especially when things went wrong.

And this was about as wrong as things could go right now.

"I think I just need a little room to breathe," she heard herself squeak.

He blinked at her in surprise, but lowered his arms. "I understand," he said sadly. "I wish to comfort you in your sorrow, but I respect your need for privacy. Please promise you will call for me when you are ready for my company again."

"O-of course," Vi said, dashing up the stairs to the third-floor landing.

Her heart felt like it was breaking, and hot tears were already running down her cheeks.

Why did he have to be so damn nice?

16

VIOLET

Vi burst in her own front door, pushed it shut and then leaned against it.

"Whoa, are you running away from someone?" Jana laughed.

Vi looked up, remembering that her roommate was home. So much for needing some space.

"Oh, Vi," Jana said, her face falling. "What happened?"

Vi appreciated that Jana didn't try to hug her. Jana understood Vi's need for autonomy. She was struck again by how lucky she was to have a friend like that.

"It wasn't Hannibal, was it?"

"No," Vi answered immediately. "Definitely not. He's awesome. It's the stupid trust. They rejected my pet grooming service."

"That sucks," Jana said. "Why? It's a great idea."

"I know, right? I already bought the truck, and I finally got it in good enough shape to drive it today," Vi moaned. "Not that I wanted to keep borrowing your car forever, but I might have chosen something other than an *ice cream truck* if I'd known I wasn't going to be using it for a mobile pet grooming service."

"At least you have good cargo space," Jana teased.

"Yes, and I get nearly four miles to the gallon on the highway," Vi said.

Jana winced.

"I'm really sorry. Speaking of ice cream, this seems like a good time to break it out."

"Yes," Vi said emphatically.

Jana always insisted on ice cream whenever one of them was feeling down. At first, Vi had been ready to dismiss the idea as just some tired cliché from the movies. But then she had tried the ice cream, and realized that there was a reason some things became clichés in the first place.

They headed into the kitchen and Vi sat while Jana fussed with bowls and spoons.

"How was your audition?" Vi asked, kicking herself for not asking sooner.

"It was fine," Jana said dismissively. "Did the trust say why the pet grooming isn't approved?"

"They said it's *unseemly*," Vi said.

"Do you really think your grandmother would have cared about that?" Jana asked.

"Definitely not," Vi said. "Remember how she made her fortune?"

"Oh yeah," Jana laughed. "Why don't you have this conversation with the trust? Remind them what your grandmother wanted, and show them you have a solid plan."

"You know that's not the worst idea," Vi mused. "It's easy to reject me on paper, but if I'm prepared, and I have an in-person meeting, maybe I'll get a different answer."

"Atta girl," Jana said.

"So were there any celebrities at your audition?" Vi

asked, knowing this would engage her friend in changing the subject.

"You know I can't say," Jana said, her eyes sparkling.

"Just give me some clues," Vi said.

"Well, I can't name names, but one of them rhymes with *Bitus Turgess.*"

"Wow!" Vi exclaimed.

"I can neither confirm nor deny," Jana said with a wink, handing Vi an enormous bowl of chocolate ice cream.

"Please tell me he's not trying out for the same part as you," Vi said.

"He'd make a great Cyndi Lauper," Jana laughed. "But no. I think I'm safe."

"So cool," Vi said with her mouth full, shaking her head and feeling infinitely better with her best friend at her side and the cold chocolate confection blossoming in her mouth.

17

HANNIBAL

Hannibal opened the door to his apartment as quietly as he could.

"Hey brother," Fletcher yelled. He was crouching on the floor, surrounded by assorted pieces of wood and gray cushions.

At least he hadn't woken anyone.

"Hello, Fletcher," Hannibal said. "What are you doing?"

"Spenser and I are building a second sofa," Fletcher replied happily. "It is in case we wish to have company. But it is not as easy as it sounds."

He and his brothers had built an interstellar spacecraft, but it was still common for them all to be confounded by the workings of much of Earth's technology. It was just so different from what they were used to. And none of them had ever had anything as clumsy as hands before.

He thought about Vi's hands, and how they hadn't seemed so clumsy as they slid along his bare skin...

"Hello, brother," Spenser said in his deep voice as he appeared in the dining room doorway, carrying a glass of water. "Where is your shirt?"

"It is in my pocket," Hannibal said, fishing it out.

He'd used it to remove most of the oil from his torso, and then thought it was better not to put it back on.

"What happened?" Fletcher asked. "Did Vi rip it off you in a fit of passion?"

Spenser hurried into the room at that comment, and sat on a chair to listen.

"Not exactly," Hannibal said sadly.

"You are mated now, are you not, brother?" Fletcher asked eagerly.

Hannibal shook his head.

"But you slept in her rooms last night," Spenser pointed out.

Hannibal nodded.

"I told her she was my mate," he said slowly.

"What did she say?" Fletcher asked.

"She seems to be attracted to me," Hannibal said.

"Well, that may be due to your form," Spenser said wisely. "That's what it's designed for, after all."

"I know, brother," Hannibal said, looking down at his body.

It was a complicated thing, with numerous vulnerabilities, but he was glad if it made Vi want to touch him.

"So what's wrong?" Spenser asked, his brow furrowed. "Why have you not sealed the bond?"

"I am not sure," Hannibal admitted. "I spoke with her, and we kissed. She wanted me. I'm sure of it. But I felt the commitment was too deep for her to decide when her judgment was clouded. So we agreed to talk today."

"I want to hear about the kissing," Fletcher said.

"How did the talk go?" Spenser interceded.

Fletcher's face fell, but he listened patiently.

"We didn't really get a chance to talk," Hannibal said.

"We intended to, but instead we ate lunch, and then Vi discovered the location of a missing dog. We spent the rest of the day locating it, and investigating the disappearance of several other dogs."

"This sounds important," Spenser said. "Perhaps it was more urgent than your conversation about mating."

"Perhaps," Hannibal agreed. "But when we reached home again, she said she needed *a little space.*"

His brothers did not reply.

They had all seen the movies that taught them Earth's culture. They knew what *a little space* meant.

"I am sorry, brother," Spenser said, rising and throwing an arm over Hannibal's shoulder. "Oh. You are greasy."

"It's a long story," Hannibal said. "I guess I'd better take a shower."

"Don't be long, brother," Fletcher said. "We have cold pizza for dinner."

"That sounds good," Hannibal said.

"And we will help you figure out what to do about your mate," Spenser added.

That sounded even better.

"I think you are wise to give her the space she needs before committing to you as a mate," Spenser said. "But do not give your friendship space. Make sure she knows you are there to support her, whether she is your mate or not. She seems like a woman who stays busy. And Dr. Bhimani says busy people can always use an extra pair of hands."

That was one of the first things Vi had said to him, when he'd met her in the hallway.

And Dr. Bhimani *did* say that. The head of the Stargazer lab was the closest thing to a parent any of the men from Aerie had. Her wisdom had led them through many mysterious situations.

It made more sense now. She didn't wish for more hands of her own. The extra hands would come from him.

He liked that idea.

"So I can stay close as long as I am useful, but I should not express my feelings," he said thoughtfully.

"This seems right, brother," Fletcher said.

That was a plan Hannibal could live with. He could not imagine separating himself from Vi, even overnight.

But he did not wish to make her unhappy by talking about their bond if she wasn't ready to talk about it.

"Thank you, brothers," Hannibal said with feeling.

He headed down the hallway toward the bathroom, but he still heard Spenser's remark to Fletcher.

"He was so greasy," Spenser whispered. "Like the pepperoni on the pizza."

"Maybe Earth women like that," Fletcher suggested.

Hannibal started the shower and thought about their advice.

Space.

He'd crossed so much of it just to get to her. He supposed he could handle a little more.

18

VIOLET

Vi was about as dressed up as she ever got.

She looked in the mirror, smoothing down her hair one last time and straightening her dress.

Impractical as it was, she did own one little black dress. Today she wore it with a grey fuzzy sweater and a pair of boots.

Jana had helped her choose the dress two years ago, explaining how Vi could wear it almost anywhere depending on how she accessorized.

But there was no way to accessorize to impress Myra Croft. Vi was just going to have to hope Myra had a full belly and a good night's sleep. Maybe then she wouldn't decide to eat Vi for breakfast.

Jana was still sleeping, so Vi slipped quietly out of the apartment, carrying a briefcase in one hand and balancing a box of grooming products on her hip.

When she reached the second-floor landing, Hannibal was waiting.

"Good morning," he said, his deep voice sending a little thrill down her spine.

"Hey," she said. "What are you doing up?"

"Waiting for you," he said simply.

Oh.

"How did you know I was going out?" she asked.

"I didn't," he admitted. "But I hoped you would not sleep late, because I missed you."

She couldn't help smiling at that and he smiled back, so handsome it almost hurt to look at him.

"Where are you going?" he asked. "Can you use an extra pair of hands?"

"Yes," she said, feeling relieved when he took the box from her.

The relief wasn't just about the box. She was glad to see him - for his own sake, and because she was about to throw herself to the wolves. It felt good to have an ally.

"We're going to talk to executor of the trust about my business," she told him as they headed downstairs. "And we don't have far to go. It's just down the block."

"That's convenient," he replied.

"Sometimes," she said.

It was beautiful outside. The sky was blue, and the big tree in front of 221B had gone from green to golden overnight. The sidewalk out front was littered with the bright yellow leaves, like rose petals on the floor of a honeymoon suite.

She tried hard not to think about honeymoon suites, and instead concentrated on the business at hand.

They reached the end of the block, crossed the street, and Vi could see the sign hanging from the doorway of their destination.

M. Croft, Esquire

She told herself she wasn't annoyed or intimidated. She was just on a business errand.

"This is it," she said when they reached the door.

"Do you want me to come in, or wait outside?" he asked.

"You can come in, but just sit in the waiting room?" she suggested.

"Perfect," he said.

She opened the door and headed in with Hannibal on her heels.

The secretary looked up from his computer and looked them over for a minute.

"How can I help you?" he said at last.

It wasn't like she'd never been here before. The man knew exactly who she was and why she was here.

"I'd like to meet with Ms. Croft," Vi said in a clear, bright voice. She wasn't going to let the man's demeanor diminish her positive attitude.

"What's this about?" he asked.

"It's about a letter I received," Vi said, a little impatiently. *Keep it together*, she chided herself.

"Ms. Croft is booked all day, you'll have to make an appointment."

"No, I don't think so," Vi said, moving past the front desk and heading for the office door.

"You can't do that," the secretary said, hopping up in alarm.

But he was too slow - Vi was already at the door. She gave a cursory knock and then opened it and stepped in.

"I'm so sorry, Ms. Croft," the secretary said petulantly.

Myra Croft looked up from the slim laptop that was open on her desk. "That's alright, Kendall," she said in a smooth, measured voice.

Vi flinched inwardly at everything implied in the tone.

Vi knew she was headstrong and determined, and she wasn't the most mannerly or fashionable.

Myra Croft always made it seem like those were unforgivable traits, like her own self-discipline and personal fashion were the only worthwhile uses of human effort.

"Go ahead, Kendall," Myra said. "Leave the door open. This won't be long."

The secretary scurried away.

"So you received my letter," Myra said in a tired way. "Go on, let's hear it. How unfair was my decision?"

"Not at all unfair," Vi replied lightly. "I assume the letter was in error."

"I assure you, it wasn't," Myra replied.

"Then I look forward to hearing your reasons for believing this business plan isn't solid without even reviewing it," Vi said.

"I don't have to make excuses to you," Myra said snippily. "It's my decision."

Vi knew she had gotten under Myra's skin now. She refrained, barely, from smiling.

"Of course it is," Vi said. "Would you like to see the data behind my business plan, so your rejection can feel more personal?"

"I wouldn't," Myra said. "Mom and Dad left me in charge, and that's that."

Vi was shocked to feel tears suddenly burn her eyes. They had lost their parents years ago. She hadn't though there was pain left in the thought.

But in this context, it still hurt, especially coming from her own sister.

"They left you in charge because you were older," Vi said. "Not because they really thought you could handle this better than I could. Think about what our grandmother wanted for us. That's the real point of all this."

"Vi, you don't understand," Myra hissed, finally losing

her cool, at least as much as she ever did, and getting out of her chair. "This idea is unseemly. Am I supposed to have my *little sister* driving around town in a van *giving pedicures to dogs?*"

"There's nothing unseemly about that," Vi retorted. "I've done the research. Everyone loves dogs. Except cold-hearted jerks."

It wasn't her best comeback, but the sentiment rang true.

"Everything you do is unseemly," Myra said. "You can't even take a day off from it. Yesterday, I send you a letter about your outrageous enterprise, today you show up with *an alien* to argue about it."

"What did you just say?" Vi asked quietly.

"I said, getting involved with an alien is so typically Violet Locke, so typically trashy and horrible."

Vi had spent a lifetime resenting her sister. Suddenly it all became clear.

They were both smart. But Myra was boring.

And she was jealous of Vi's ability to follow her interests.

"If you think marrying that snooze-fest Ed Croft makes you better than me, you're more delusional than I thought," Vi said, her voice gradually rising as her anger gained momentum. "I like who I am. If pretending to be like you is the only way for me to unlock that trust, well... You can take your money and *stuff it in a sack.*"

Vi tried to memorize the visual of her sister's perfectly lip-glossed mouth as it opened and then closed again. It might have been the first time in her entire life that Myra had nothing to say.

Then Vi turned on her heel and headed out.

19

HANNIBAL

Hannibal stood in the waiting room, his heart overflowing as Vi's words echoed in his head.

You can take your money and stuff it in a sack.

She had chosen him.

Whether she knew it or not, Vi had just found peace in being herself.

And Hannibal knew the strength of their bond meant that being herself meant accepting him as her own.

He might be new to this planet, but he was aware of the way Vi viewed herself. It was impossible to miss the occasions when she cringed at her own leadership tendencies, the way she looked at her friend as if Jana had figured out a better way to be a woman.

He hadn't been able to understand how someone so strong, so smart, and so beautiful could question her own value.

But now that he knew that the woman in the other room was her sister, he began to see things in a different way.

If Vi's parents had shown preference for her sister's less

demonstrative personality and more material lifestyle, then no wonder Vi thought others might share that preference. If there was one thing Hannibal had learned about humans, it was that the parenting of offspring was of utmost importance.

He couldn't wait for Vi to come out so that he could tell her how proud he was to have her for his mate.

But when she appeared in the threshold her confidence was so great, she almost seemed to be glowing.

She did not need to hear his opinion.

Vi was proud to be herself.

And that was all he could wish for.

"Vi," he said, overcome.

She strode up to him, dropped the box at her feet, and went up on her toes to kiss him.

Just before her lips touched his, her phone made a terrible sound.

She pulled back and dug around frantically in her pocket.

"What is that?" Hannibal asked.

"It's a nine-one-one text," she gasped, finding the phone at last.

"You work for emergency services?" Hannibal asked, stunned.

"No, no," she said. "When a friend texts that, it means they need your help right away. And the friend who needs us right away is Micah."

Hannibal's joy dissipated instantly.

He had only known his landlords a few days, but already they felt like family. Hannibal had never had a family emergency before.

"Let's go," he said.

He took Vi's hand and together they ran down the block for home.

"Wait," the secretary called after them. "You left all your stuff."

"I'll get it later," Vi yelled back. "This is more important."

20

VIOLET

Vi saw the police cars and the ambulance out front of their home, and sprinted for the front door with Hannibal by her side.

"*Micah*," she screamed as the headed to the door to Tony and Micah's apartment.

The door was open.

Micah sat on the sofa, a blanket around his shoulders.

Tony sat by his side, a calming hand on his husband's back.

Fletcher and Spenser stood next to the sofa, as if guarding it. Spenser's eyes were fixed on Officer West, who stood by the window, jotting on a small notepad. She seemed to be deliberately avoiding eye contact with Spenser. Or maybe Vi was just imagining that part. She made a mental note to ask Hannibal about it later.

"What happened?" Vi demanded as she burst in.

"Your friend here called emergency services and an ambulance for a missing dog," the officer replied.

Micah cringed a bit at that, tears streaking his face.

"He didn't call an ambulance," Tony said firmly.

Officer West picked up her notebook.

"He said, '*She's gone, my heart, my heart.*' And when the operator asked who was gone, he said, '*My baby is gone. Maybelle is gone.*' And when they asked how old she was, he said, '*She's ten. My heart, my heart. Please find her. I think I'm going to die.*' Did I get that right, sir?"

"Everything I said was one hundred percent accurate," Micah said, nodding, but looking a little sheepish.

"So you can see why I showed up here with an ambulance," West explained.

"Hey," Vi said, striding over. "Maybe you should start looking for the dog, instead of browbeating my friend."

"It might surprise you to hear this," West retorted. "But the police sometimes have more important things to do than track down missing pets and quell farmer's market PA system disruptions."

Actually, it did surprise Vi a little. What else ever happened in Stargazer that was so urgent? The biggest case of the past six months had to do with some kids stealing change out of a broken parking meter. She decided it was best not to let Officer West know how she felt.

"There are a lot of missing dogs in this town," Vi said instead. "Aren't you worried about it?"

"Listen, Miss Locke," Officer West said. "I already got an earful about you once today. I'm not really in the mood for any more."

"Why would anyone be talking to you about me?" Vi asked.

"I called Joanne Griffin about her missing dog, and she was quick to tell me all about how you found it, and how much more effective Violet Locke is than the worthless Stargazer police," West said coldly.

"Oh," Vi replied, shocked.

"She said the guy down the street was talking with your boyfriend about his missing pet, too," West went on. "Now it's got me thinking, why are you two so wrapped up in this? You don't even have a pet."

Vi was speechless.

"Maybe *you* know where all the missing dogs are and you just want to be a hero, get a little attention," West suggested. "Maybe you're looking for a publicity stunt to drum up customers for your that new business. You want to talk about it some more? Maybe we should do it down at the station."

"That's enough," Hannibal said.

His voice was low and level but as firm as granite.

"We'll look for your dog, Mr. Delago," West said to Micah in a subdued voice.

Micah nodded and clutched Tony's hand.

"Do us all a favor, and stay out of the way," West hissed to Vi on the way out.

There was a moment of silence and then Vi turned to Micah.

"Where was the last place you saw Maybelle?" Vi asked, getting right to business. Jana and the boys could do the comforting. Vi knew how crucial the first few hours were in a missing person situation.

"I left her in the garden, just for a moment," Micah said. "I had to get my bag because we were going shopping."

"The garden is walled," Vi said.

Micah nodded.

"And I knew she was out there because she barked at the mail man. One minute she was giving him the business, the next there was only silence."

He bit his lip and Tony pulled him close.

The door swung open and Jana ran in. "What's going on? What happened?"

Tony gave her the rundown, and she sat on the other side of Micah, taking his hand.

Jana reached for her purse.

"What is that noise?" Fletcher asked.

"Wait," Jana said. "You can hear that?"

"I can hear it," Hannibal said.

"What are you talking about?" Tony asked, sharing a confused look with Micah.

"I hear it, too," Spenser added.

Vi heard nothing, but she didn't need to hear it to know exactly what they were talking about.

"Impressive," Jana said, taking her phone out of the purse and ignoring an incoming call.

"What do you mean?" Fletcher asked.

"The tone you just heard is my phone ringing," Jana explained. "Because of my work, I get a lot of super early phone calls about auditions, and I don't want to disturb anyone. I've always had really good ears. So I chose what they call a mosquito tone. Kid's use them in school to fake out the teachers. Certain tones can only be heard if you're below a certain age. It's something about the frequency. This one is supposed to be audible only to people under the age of twenty-four - though I can still hear it because my ears are in good shape. This way, when my phone rings, I'm the only one in the house who can hear it. Until now, I guess. Did I explain that right, Vi?"

But the conversation had tickled Vi's brain and she was already deep in thought.

"I've got it," Vi yelled as the final piece clicked together. "We're going to use a high-pitched tone to find the dogs."

"What?" Jana asked.

"Like my whistle," Hannibal said, his eyes lighting up.

"Yes, and my sound equipment," Vi said. "We'll go out to where we found Sassafras and play a tone just like your whistle plays. We'll see if we can get the dogs to tell us where they are."

Vi loved the new plan already. Dogs were so much more reliable than people.

21

VIOLET

Vi drove, her thoughts laser focused on the task at hand.

Hannibal sat in the passenger seat beside her, and the others squeezed together on the bench seat in the back of the truck.

"Wow, we're like the Scooby gang, aren't we?" Jana whispered.

"Kind of," Vi said. "But we don't have a dog and we're really winging it."

"Like Scooby Doo?" Fletcher asked Jana. "Do you think the culprit is really one of the townsfolk wearing a mask?"

Hannibal recalled the adventures of the heroic dog and his human sidekicks fondly. They had all found his antics very enjoyable.

"Not exactly," Jana told him. "But just wait. I bet these meddling kids are going to blow the case wide open."

"We are the meddling kids!" Fletcher announced, and then shared a hearty laugh with Jana.

Hannibal seemed glad to see his brother having such pleasant interactions with Vi's best friend. And Vi was well aware of the way they looked at each other when they thought no one was watching.

It was very cute. And she loved seeing Jana happy.

She only hoped his brother Spenser might find someone better to connect with. So far, the only woman who had sparked Spenser's interest seemed to be Officer West, who was quite lovely and capable in her own right, but too often at odds with Vi. That could turn out to be very problematic.

"Here we are," Vi said, grabbing everyone's attention.

They had reached the intersection with Lindbergh Lane, right around where they had found Sassafras.

"I'm just going to pull over and turn on the equipment," Vi said.

"No need," Hannibal told her.

He closed his eyes in concentration, and then opened them a moment later.

"It's playing," he told her.

They would have to take his word for it. Even Jana couldn't hear the dog whistle tone.

"Roll down your windows," Vi advised Hannibal as she lowered hers.

"Roll it down?" he asked, studying it doubtfully.

"Sorry, press the button to make the glass slide down," she said.

He did as she asked.

"Everybody listen," Vi instructed as she began driving slowly down the lane.

They got close to the red barn where she and Hannibal had gone last night. Her thoughts began to drift to the feel of his rock-hard body under her slick hands, but the sound of distant barking snapped her mind back to the present.

"Oh my gosh," Jana murmured.

Vi drove on, following the sound further down Lindbergh.

The barking grew louder she reached the abandoned stables about a quarter of a mile down the road, with more dogs joining the chorus. She pulled the van over and cut the engine. There was no mistaking it. The dogs were in there somewhere.

"We have to be smart about this," she whispered to the others. "We have no idea what we're up against."

Hannibal nodded.

"If we all go, we will make too much noise," Vi said. "Jana, can you, Fletcher and Spenser stay in the van and be ready to join us if we give the signal?"

"Sure, what's the signal?" Jana asked.

"A super loud whistle, at human frequency," Vi said.

"Why don't we just call the police and get them to check it out?" Jana asked.

"You heard Officer West. The police aren't exactly happy with me right now," Vi reminded her. "And besides, they're not taking this dog thing seriously. If we call them, the dog-nappers could be long gone by the time they decide to check it out. We need to catch them in the act."

Jana buttoned her lips, but she nodded.

"Okay, here we go," Vi said, nodding to Hannibal.

They got out of the van and headed for the stable.

It was dark, but the moonlight allowed Vi to see just enough to move quickly and quietly.

The old sign for the abandoned stables had a picture of a horse with a seahorse's body, the paint was peeling off, but she could just make out the name *Seahorse Stables*. They must have missed the memo about everything in town following a space motif.

The door to the first stable stood partly open, so Vi slipped in, with Hannibal right behind her.

The sound of barking was much louder. The dogs were somewhere among the abandoned buildings on this farm.

Vi took off running, hoping to get to the dogs before whoever was keeping them figured out what was afoot.

They came out the back of the stable and into an open courtyard between two other stables, just below the white farmhouse on the ridge above.

Vi caught movement ahead of her. Someone was coming down from the farmhouse, heading toward one of the stables.

"He's making a run for it," she gasped to Hannibal, pushing herself to move faster.

Clearly this person had the advantage of knowing the terrain. It would be horrible to lose their top suspect when they were so close.

She swung toward the stable on the right. Inside, darkened bulbs hung from the ceiling, but there was no switch in sight. The sound of the barking echoed off the stall walls, making it hard to concentrate on finding the human.

But whoever was behind the dog-nappings needed to be caught, or else Vi could free these animals and more would just go missing tomorrow.

She whistled as loudly as she could, hoping the others would hear and come to help.

Now that she knew the dogs were here, they needed extra hands more than they needed stealth, or a speedy getaway.

She scanned the stalls, but she couldn't hear any footsteps over the howling dogs.

"Hannibal," she said, turning to him. "Can you get the lights on?"

He closed his eyes and for an instant she was reminded how beautiful he was, how magical...

Then the lights went on all at once, so brightly it almost seemed that the bulbs would burst.

And in the corner, she saw a huge man, cowering.

"Darwin Brody?" Vi whispered in awe.

The man straightened and she saw that she was right. Darwin was a former professional football player who had recently moved to Stargazer. It had been a great human-interest story at the time. Darwin had said on the local news that despite his fame, he'd always felt like a bit of an outsider, and that any town with so many aliens would be a likely spot for a big guy like him to fit in.

The residents had eaten it up.

"Yes," Darwin said. "What are you doing here?"

"What are *you* doing here?" Vi countered.

"I own this place," Darwin said. "I'm opening up shop as a dog trainer."

"That's right," Vi remembered out loud. She had heard something about that on the radio. She just hadn't known that he had bought the old stables. "Why did you run from us?"

"Because you were trespassing on my farm after dark and you scared the living daylights out of me," Darwin said.

"That tracks," Vi agreed, wondering if one day she'd tell her grandchildren she met the great Darwin Brody and frightened him because he'd mistaken her for a prowler.

Actually, there was no mistake - she *was* a prowler.

"So why are you here?" Darwin asked, putting it all together at the same time she had.

"We're looking for missing dogs," Hannibal answered. "One of the dogs on the missing posters in town was found half a block from here, and we had a hunch."

"You found Sassafras?" Darwin asked, hope in his eyes.

"Yes, we found him," Vi said. "He's back with his owner. You know you can't just steal people's pets, even just to train them. Although you did a hell of job. He was so well-behaved that she thought it wasn't even her dog."

"He really made progress, didn't he?" Darwin said fondly. "But I didn't steal them. They were delivered here."

"What do you mean delivered?" Vi asked.

"An Über driver showed up with them," Darwin said. "Told me the owner wanted them all trained and that he valued his privacy. The driver had an envelope of cash for me and said someone would be back in two weeks to pick them up."

"That's the craziest thing I've ever heard," Vi said.

Darwin shrugged.

"I don't know, a lot of my former teammates have a bunch of pets. I'm not one to judge. Animals rock. And I get it that some people want their privacy."

"You value your privacy," Vi thought out loud. "Do you come to town often?"

"Not really," Darwin admitted. "I'll come more when people get used to having me here. Sometimes I just want to be myself you know? I don't always feel like giving auto-graphs or reminiscing about games. It's one of the reasons I moved away from the city."

"That's why you didn't see the missing dog signs all over town," Vi said.

"I guess not. Look, this is getting kind of intense," Darwin said. "Maybe we can call the police and let them know what's going on. Find the owners of all these dogs? I definitely didn't buy this place just to get involved in an illegal dog-napping ring. I'm not Michael Vick."

"We know that," Hannibal said kindly. "I am Hannibal, and this is Vi."

"Nice to meet you," Darwin said, offering Hannibal his hand.

Vi heard Jana calling her name as the sound of numerous footsteps entered the stable.

"Back here," Vi called to their friends. "We found them."

"I'll call Micah," Jana said happily.

"And I'll call Officer West," Vi said, less happily.

22

HANNIBAL

Hannibal watched as Maybelle scampered down the hallway to Tony and Micah's apartment. Vi grabbed his hand and they followed along to witness the happy reunion.

Micah cried and clutched the little dog to his big chest as she licked his nose again and again in obvious delight.

"I can't believe it," Tony said, running over to shake Vi's hand and then Hannibal's and then Vi's again. "You found her. We're so grateful."

"She wasn't the only one we found," Hannibal said.

Tony looked around for a moment.

"But they're all home now," Vi added.

"Who was behind it?" Tony asked.

"That's the odd thing," Vi said. "We don't know. Someone brought them to a training facility."

"Excuse me, what?" Micah asked, looking up just in time for Maybelle to lick him on the chin.

"You know Darwin Brody, the football player?" Vi asked.

"Not really," Micah said, raising one eyebrow. "I'm not a big football fan, except for those little pants."

"You know him," Tony scolded. "He was in that Mother's Day soup commercial a couple of years ago that made you cry."

"Ohhhh, sure," Micah said. "What about him?"

"Well, he's living in Stargazer now and he's starting up business as a dog trainer," Vi said. "He told us that someone showed up with a bunch of dogs and said that the owner wanted them trained."

"Get out of town," Micah said. "Do you know tricks now, Maybelle?"

Maybelle stopped licking his cheek and cocked her head to the side as if she were trying to hear him.

"Lie down," Micah said.

Maybelle flopped down on his lap.

"Oh my God," Micah exclaimed. "Get up, get up and kiss me."

"Well, that's neat but it won't last long," Tony confided. "We live to spoil her."

"Who could blame you?" Vi asked. "I'm not normally a pet person, but she's a special pup."

Tony smiled at her, clearly charmed.

Hannibal's heart ached with love for Vi.

"So what are you kids up to tonight?" Micah asked, tearing his eyes from Maybelle long enough to look back and forth between them. "Now that you've saved the day, that is."

"No idea," Vi said. "But it had better involve food."

"Our getaway," Micah suggested.

"Oh, good thinking," Tony said.

"What getaway?" Vi asked.

"Micah and I like to treat ourselves once every couple of months," Tony said. "So when the Stargazer Suites runs a discount, we snag a night at the penthouse and gorge on room service and then soak in the hot tub all night."

"Nice," Vi said.

"We booked a non-refundable deal for tonight," Tony said. "But when Maybelle went missing..."

"We'll watch her for you," Vi offered at once. "It'll be fun."

"No, no, no, honey," Micah said, standing up with Maybelle in his arms. "We're not going anywhere. But you and Hannibal should take the penthouse for the night."

"Oh, we couldn't," Vi said.

"We insist," Tony told her. "If you don't, it will sit empty. They have a strict no pets policy. And there's no way Micah is letting Maybelle out of his sight."

"Besides, we owe you big time for finding Maybelle," Micah added. "You deserve some pampering."

Vi looked at Hannibal and he nodded.

"It's a deal," she said.

An hour later, Hannibal found himself sitting on a gigantic bed, surrounded by half-eaten plates of extremely fancy food.

"They weren't kidding about gorging themselves," Vi said, leaning back with a satisfied look. "This is an insane amount of food."

"I don't think I've ever failed to finish a meal before," Hannibal said, feeling a little defeated.

"This is not a meal," Vi said encouragingly. "This is a feast. Eating it all would have been a bad idea."

He nodded.

She was right, but human food was such a pleasure that he didn't understand how they didn't spend all their time eating.

"On Aerie it took all day to soak in enough starlight to fuel oneself," he said dreamily.

"I guess the human way of eating leaves more room for other activities," Vi said.

Her words were spoken in innocence, but they stoked a fire in him. There were so many other ways in which he would like to spend his time with Vi.

"We have had full days since I told you about the bond," he said carefully. "But have you had ample time to give it thought?"

"What do you mean?" she asked.

"Have you decided?" he asked nervously. "Might you choose to be my mate?"

She blinked at him and he felt a cold like the blackest void of space descend on him.

"Of course I'll be your mate," she said at last. "Unless you're having second thoughts?"

Warmth ran through him again and he crawled past a stack of plates to her, cupping her hand in his palm.

"I could not have second thoughts if I wanted to," he told her solemnly. "And I would never want to. You are brave and wise, you will be an ideal parent for our young."

"Our young?" she echoed.

"Of course," he said. "We will raise a pack of smart, inventive children. But we don't need to grow our family right away. I'd like to enjoy you for a long time first."

She smiled at him looking surprised.

"Did I say something wrong?" he asked.

"No," she said. "The opposite. I-I never really thought about having a baby before."

"You didn't?" he asked.

He had thought all human females dreamed of being mothers, but he sensed this was a wrong statement. He was beginning to understand that no two humans were more than marginally similar.

And he was glad Vi was just as she was. Even if not having young was a sad thought.

"But something about the way you put it," she continued. "I don't know. It kind of sounds cool. Like an adventure."

He leaned in and kissed her nose.

"Now listen," she said. "I know that to make all this official, we have to... you know. Jump in bed."

He smiled. They were already in bed. What they had to do was make love and give their bodies to their bond as they had their hearts.

"Do you not wish to *jump in bed* with me, Violet Locke?" he asked.

She gulped, her pupils dilating slightly, telling him she felt desire.

Gods but he enjoyed her responses to him.

"I do wish to jump in bed with you," she whispered back huskily. "But, well, I've been around the block, I guess, but I'm not... good at it."

He blinked and tried to understand what those words might mean.

"Jumping in bed," she clarified. "I haven't done it that much and never with someone I... cared about the way I care about you. I don't want to mess it up. I don't want you to be disappointed."

He drew back and examined her face.

She was embarrassed.

"Vi, I have never *jumped in bed* with anyone before," he told her. "We will learn together."

"I guess I never thought about that," she admitted.

"Well, let's not think about it," he told her. "Let's go swimming instead."

She laughed and suddenly she was his Vi again, fearless.

They piled up the dishes on a tray and placed it on a table beside the bed.

Then Hannibal slowly peeled off his t-shirt.

Vi's eyes widened.

He grinned at her and slid his jeans down slowly.

Vi hid her face in her hands.

"Your turn," he told her.

"No way, I want to see the rest of this show," she teased.

He obliged her, removing everything until he stood before her naked.

He felt her eyes rake over every inch of his form, like she was touching him, and his body roared to life at the thought of it.

"Now you," he growled. "Or do you need help?"

She shook her head and began to undress, slowly.

He watched, welcoming the sight of her arms, her breasts, the curve of her belly meeting her hips, her round bottom, and the adorable dimples in her thighs.

At last she stood before him, naked and strong.

His love. His mate.

Hannibal's heart was full.

She smiled at him and he went to her.

He pulled her body against his, reveling in her softness, the perfect way her small form melted into his.

She wrapped her arms around his neck, and he carried her to the bed.

"What about swimming?" she whispered.

"First I need to taste you," he told her.

She shivered in his arms and he fought against the pull

of his body. He had to be patient, to show her that they could be good at this.

He laid her down and crawled in beside her.

She gazed up at him, her eyes luminous.

"I want to touch you now, Violet," he told her. "Tell me if I need to stop."

She closed her eyes in assent.

He pressed his lips to hers, gently at first, then more passionately as she kissed him back.

For a long time he tasted her lips, her tongue.

When he could feel her heart pounding like his, he pressed one last kiss to the corner of her mouth and trailed his lips across her cheek to nibble her earlobe.

Vi laughed suddenly and he pulled back.

"Was that funny?" he asked, confused. In the movies, women liked to be kissed on their ear.

"No," she said. "It feels nice. It just tickles."

"I will resume," he told her.

This time he licked her earlobe into his mouth and suckled gently.

She sighed and arched her back, as if she wanted more.

He trailed kisses down her neck, nuzzling her clavicle and made his way to her breasts.

"You are so beautiful," he told her.

She blushed and then smiled at him.

He curled one palm around her breast, swiping the pad of his thumb upward to feel the delicate texture of her nipple.

Vi was watching him, her lips slightly parted and swollen from his kisses.

He leaned down slowly and flicked his tongue against the little bead.

Vi's head fell back against the pillow and she made a small, wanting sound.

Encouraged, he tasted her again, lapping at one nipple and then the other, sucking and nibbling gently until she arched her back and her hips trembled under him.

"Hannibal," she murmured.

"Is it good, my love?" he asked her.

"Yes," she sighed.

He kissed her belly and her hips, then moved lower.

Vi was pressing her thighs tightly together, but when he nuzzled the place where they met, she relaxed and allowed him access.

He brushed his lips against the tender insides of her thighs even as his body burned to take her.

The sight and scent of her sex were overwhelming.

Be calm. Be patient, he warned himself.

But it was so hard to be patient.

When he pressed his lips to her opening, she cried out and he could feel her thighs tense.

He licked her where he had kissed her before, parting her, tasting the spicy sweetness of her.

Violet moaned and the sound drove him wild.

He fell on her, licking, sucking, and searching for the little kernel he knew would bring her pleasure crashing down on her, reveling in the stiff, smoothness of it when at last his tongue found her. He goaded her toward paradise, flicking and lapping at the little pearl.

Vi was gasping and whimpering now, her hips lifting slightly as if to meet his mouth.

She was ready.

23

VIOLET

Vi was floating, practically out of her body with the pleasure.

Hannibal had her on the razor's edge, and all she could think about was the next stroke of his tongue.

When he pulled back, she nearly cried.

But he was crawling up to press his body to hers.

She wrapped her arms around him, kissing him and tasting her own excitement on his lips.

"Vi, are you sure?" His voice was raspy and low with lust.

"Yes," she said simply.

He guided himself against her, gazing into her eyes as he pressed slowly inside until he was fully seated.

The pleasure was enough to blot out the pinch of him stretching her. Vi sank her nails into his biceps and lifted her hips to meet him.

He gasped and thrust into her again, muscles straining.

She heard a low moan and was surprised to realize it was her own desperate sound.

"Please," she whimpered.

Suddenly he was moving faster, giving her the long,

steady strokes her body craved, pushing her higher and higher until the ecstasy tugged her like a helium balloon.

She jogged her hips, desperate for the spark that would ignite her ecstasy.

Hannibal slid his hand between them, found her nodule again and worked it gently with his fingers.

Vi closed her eyes and the ecstasy exploded. It wasn't just one part of her, it felt like her entire body was suffused with warm light until the pleasure shot out from her fingers and her hair.

Hannibal groaned and she felt him swell impossibly inside her. Then his own pleasure was jetting from him while hers was still swirling in a shared ecstasy that seemed to go on forever.

At last, he collapsed beside her, pulling her onto his chest. She felt the exact moment the bond was sealed and Hannibal *clicked* permanently into his human form. She couldn't explain it, but it was almost like he was somehow more *there* than before. And like there was something more to her than there had ever been.

She closed her eyes, meaning to rest just for a moment.

"I love you, Violet Locke," he whispered into her hair.

"I love you too, Hannibal," she whispered back.

She was so excited that she was sure sleep would elude her, but with his warm arms wrapped around her, she found herself drifting.

24

VIOLET

The next day, Vi sat on the patio with Jana and Micah, sipping tea and watching the men help Tony in the garden while Maybelle alternately napped and chased the leaves and sticks the guys were kicking up.

It was a gorgeous fall afternoon, and watching her mate and his brothers laugh while they trimmed branches and raked leaves was about the best way to spend it that Vi could imagine.

"Oh listen, here's another one," Micah said, reading from his phone. *"Violet Locke and her boyfriend Stanbull brought back my Daisy, which is more than I can say for the so-called professional Stargazer police force. They wouldn't even accept a reward."*

"Who is Stanbull?" Jana teased. "Should Hannibal be worried?"

Vi laughed.

"Worried about what?" Hannibal called back to them from where he was bundling a pile of sticks.

"You don't ever have to worry about anything," Vi called back to him.

"Awwwww," Micah and Jana crooned in unison.

He smiled and went back to work.

Vi turned to Jana to see if her friend thought Hannibal was as irresistible as she did.

But Jana was staring openly at Fletcher as he peeled off his t-shirt and tossed it onto the garden wall.

"Oh, wow, this one's not about you," Micah said.

"What is it?" Vi asked, secretly glad not to hear any more community board posts about herself.

"Sounds like someone stole Herman Wendall's cars," Micah said.

"Who in the world would want those cars?" Vi asked, incredulous.

Herman Wendall had three ancient clunkers on bricks in his front yard, like a quintessential movie hillbilly. The irony was that Herman was a very successful accountant and he had a perfectly good car that he drove into the village each day for work. He had it in his mind that fixing up the old cars would be a fun hobby, but he never seemed to get around to finishing one. Or starting one, as far as Vi could tell.

Which was a shame, since the little purple Corvette Stingray seemed like it would be pretty sweet.

The cars were a source of amusement and distress to his neighbors, depending on which one you asked.

"Who knows why people do anything?" Micah said. "Oh, wait, it's not entirely without a mention of you after all. Someone in the comments is saying he ought to call Violet and Sansom. Why can no one get Hannibal's name right?"

Vi shrugged.

Her phone rang and she slid it out of her pocket.

Myra. Great.

Against her better judgement, she swiped to pick up. Her mood was too good right now for even her sister to ruin.

"Yeah?" she said, getting out of her chair and walking to the other side of the patio.

"Listen, Vi, you left your stuff here," Myra said.

"You can throw it out," Vi said swiftly.

"No," Myra said. "I mean, that's not why I called."

"What do you want, Myra?" Vi asked, wondering if she had overestimated her ability to resist her sister's negativity.

"I read your plan," Myra said. "It's actually quite good. Very well thought out and thoroughly researched."

"You don't say," Vi said, trying to maintain an air of sarcasm despite being absolutely floored. A compliment from her sister was the rarest of creatures.

"I think it could work," Myra went on. "And you're right, Grandma was certainly not snobby when she chose her business. You can probably make money at this. I'm changing my decision. This enterprise counts."

"Forget about it," Vi said. "I don't want to do it anymore."

There was silence on the line long enough that Vi wondered if her phone had dropped the call.

"What are you talking about?" Myra asked at last.

"I'm saying it's a good plan, but it's not something I actually want to do," Vi said.

"So you're telling me you don't care about the trust anymore? You don't care about having money?" Myra asked, her frustration coming through.

"I don't know what I want right now," Vi said. "But it's not that."

"Oh, I get it," Myra said with a sarcastic laugh. "You found a couple of missing dogs and now what? You think you're a private detective?"

"What did you just say?" Vi asked.

"You know what? I regret calling you," Myra said. "Good luck finding your bliss, or whatever it is that motivates you."

"Yeah, yeah," Vi said distractedly and hung up.

A private detective.

"Is everything okay?" Hannibal jogged up to her.

"That was my sister," she said. "And yes, everything is fine."

"Good," he said, pulling her close and kissing the top of her head.

"She said she would approve the pet grooming business," Vi said. "But I don't want to do it anymore."

"That makes sense," Hannibal said. "It doesn't seem like it would hold your interest."

"But it would mean a lot of money," Vi said.

"Do we need a lot of money?" he asked.

Vi looked around at their friends, enjoying the small garden and each other's company. If she was being completely honest with herself, she didn't need more than this.

"I guess not," she said.

"Because I can probably get plenty of money if you need it," he added. "Everyone wants aliens for something called *endorsement deals*. Dr. Bhimani promised to help me look over any contracts I might get."

"No, no," Vi said. "We don't need that kind of money. I'd rather live simply and do something interesting."

"Like what?" he asked.

"How would you feel about driving around in an old ice cream truck and solving mysteries?" Vi asked.

"As long as it's with you, I don't care what I'm doing," Hannibal said. "But that sounds really fun."

Vi felt a wave of love for him that almost knocked her off her feet.

She went up on her toes to kiss him.

He wrapped his arms around her and kissed her back, intoxicating her with the warmth and scent of his big body, even as she knew it was his kind and open heart that was truly his best feature.

At last he pulled away.

"Vi, there's something I have to ask you," he said.

"Okay," she said, wondering why he didn't just ask.

Then suddenly he was down on one knee, holding her hand, lifting up something tiny that gleamed in the sunlight.

"Violet Locke, will you marry me?" he asked.

She could hear Jana gasp and Tony drop the garden shears he was holding.

"Oh my God," Micah whispered loudly. Out of the corner of her eye she could see him lifting his phone to make a video.

At first glance, it might have seemed like it wasn't the most romantic setting Hannibal could have chosen, but as far as Vi was concerned, sharing this moment with their friends was absolutely perfect.

"Yes," she laughed. "Yes, of course."

Then he was on his feet again, slipping the ring on her finger and hugging her close as their friends ran over to congratulate them.

The world might be full of mystery. But when it came to what was important, Vi was finally beginning to feel like she had it all figured out.

***

Thanks for reading **Hannibal!**

Want to see what happens when Hannibal's brother and Vi's best friend suddenly find themselves a LOT closer than they ever planned? Jana is finally getting her big break as an actress, what will she do when she finds out she's destined to be the mate to alien of her dreams? Just keep reading to get a sample of Jana and Fletcher's story...

Or grab your copy now!

Fletcher: Stargazer Alien Mystery Brides #2

https://www.tashablack.com/samysterybrides.html

FLETCHER - SAMPLE

1

JANA

J ana Watson was dreaming.

She knew it from the sight of the beach - the cool blue ocean and the snowy white sand, baking under a hot afternoon sun.

She had spent every summer at the same beach as a kid, until her family lost everything but each other in the recession.

The house at the Jersey shore was nothing special, as her mom had told her repeatedly. They'd bought it cheap, meaning to fix it up one day, and the bank had taken it instead.

But Jana didn't think about the paneled walls and the chipped formica counters. When she recalled *the house down the shore,* she remembered the creak of the porch swing and the way the painted floor boards clung slightly to her bare feet like kisses in the humidity.

To Jana, it had been the most magical place in the world.

When she made it big, she was going to buy it back, or a place just like it. Whenever things got stressful, she closed her eyes and pictured herself here.

But it never felt so real as it did right now.

The sand was hot enough to almost burn the soles of her feet, and the scent and sight of the ocean filled her with a feeling of smallness she hadn't experienced in so long.

She looked out past the waves at the place where the sky and sea melted into each other and shivered with delight. Jana took a step toward the water and a salty breeze whipped by, carrying her straw hat with it.

She turned to see it tumbling across the sand. And though she knew the wind and gravity alternately controlled it, it felt as if some other thing were pulling it too. It was as if the hat were on marionette strings so that some unseen force could draw it into the tall grasses.

She chased it lazily, half-watching its progress. When it found a lively air current and sailed over her head, she spun around, back toward the beach.

The sun was sinking now, glittering on the water and setting the waves into bold relief. Its brilliance made her blink against the sight before her.

A man stood, silhouetted against the shimmering ocean.

He was holding her hat.

Jana shielded her eyes with her hand and tried got get a look at him.

The shape of him was familiar somehow. He was huge and muscular, yet his posture was not menacing.

He looked like he was waiting for her. Like he would patiently wait lifetimes...

"Fletcher?" she whispered, knowing him by his gentle presence more than his physical features. Although his sandy hair and deep blue eyes seemed like a perfect echo of their surroundings.

He moved toward her, slowly enough that she could change her mind if she wanted.

But Jana's body and soul were ready to surrender to her need for him, which felt heavy as an anchor, inexorable as the setting of the sun over the water.

"Jana," he murmured, taking her in his arms.

His chest was warm and she could feel the flex of his muscles as his arms closed around her.

Just as she had always imagined.

She shivered with pleasure as he nuzzled her hair.

"Jana," he murmured again. "Jana."

His voice was pitching strangely higher now.

No, no, no...

"Jana."

The dream was ending. Already, she could feel her pillow wrapped in her arms instead of his strong body, the cool sheet beneath her instead of the hot sand.

"*Jana, it's time to go,*" came Vi's impatient voice from the other side of the door.

"I'm up," Jana managed. "I'm up, just give me a minute."

"Awesome," Vi said approvingly. "You have twenty minutes."

If she had twenty minutes, Jana would have much preferred to spend it seeing where that dream was going.

But there was no point arguing with Vi. Jana's amazing roommate had made the decision to give up on her mobile pet grooming business and hang a shingle as a private detective instead. And Jana, having nothing else to do while she awaited the results of her second Broadway callback, had volunteered to be her Girl Friday.

She dragged herself out of bed and headed to her bathroom for a quick shower.

Twenty minutes later on the dot, Jana was dressed and ready with a cup of coffee in hand, sitting at the picnic table on the shared patio behind their building.

Vi had a cup of coffee too, but she had to keep putting it down because she talked with her hands.

"It could be a very long morning," Vi was warning Jana. "We have no idea when he's going to take the truck out."

"Isn't that kind of the whole deal with a stakeout?" Jana asked.

"Yeah, but I wasn't sure you knew," Vi said.

"Only from the movies, but I think I'm good," Jana said. "I brought a thermos of coffee, and..." She pulled a pair of sunglasses out of her bag and slid them on. "These."

Vi burst out laughing.

"What?" Jana asked. "I just got them. You don't like them?"

"No, no, they're great," Vi said. "It's just... you're the only person I know who can put on a pair of sunglasses and look *less* incognito."

Well, there was nothing Jana could do about that.

"I guess it's not your fault you're gorgeous," Vi said, shaking her head. "I'm going in to grab my bag. Stay here a minute."

Jana laughed and watched her go. There was a time when that whole exchange would have given her a stomachache.

Jana was tall and curvy, even her dark eyes were larger than life. What she would have given to have her friend's less conspicuous appearance back in high school.

She had always been told she was beautiful, but a quick glance at a magazine flipped that idea on its head. Compared to those images, everything about Jana was excessive - too tall, too heavy, even too loud. Or at least that was the impression she got from them.

Ironically, it was a teenaged summer begrudgingly spent at Theatre camp because there were no spaces left at Art camp, that had given Jana the escape she needed from worrying about being herself.

At first, she had been more self-conscious than ever, standing on the stage, wishing she could disappear - or failing that, that at least thirty percent of her could disappear.

Then Mr. Lafferty had taken notice of her. No matter what else was going on, he would call out to her, "No slouching, Jana," or "Stand tall, Jana," or, everyone's favorite, "Own it, Jana!"

And once she could stand up tall and proud on the stage while the other kids cheered her on, it was suddenly easier to picture standing up tall at home and at school. She floated through the rest of summer, loving her new lease on life.

On the last day of camp Mr. Lafferty pulled her aside.

"Jana," he said, "I'm proud of you. And I think you've got talent. You may have a future in theatre if you're willing to work hard."

"I don't know," she'd said, shrugging.

It was one thing for your school friends to tell you to own it. It was another to compete in a field full of critical strangers, where looks were everything.

"Who is the target audience in live theatre?" Mr. Lafferty had asked.

"I don't know," Jana said again, but this time with interest. She had never really thought about that. "Everyone?"

"Sure," Mr. Lafferty said. "Everyone is welcome at the theatre. But the patrons who spend the most, donate the most, and spread the word the most are women, age forty to sixty."

"Yeah?" Jana asked, wondering what he could possibly be trying to tell her.

"Women age forty to sixty don't give a damn about whether you're an emaciated waif or a curvy starlet" Mr. Lafferty said, impressing her by dropping a curse word. "They just want to see good theatre. But they have something going against them."

Yeah, women have half the world going against them, Jana thought to herself.

"Do you know what it is?" Mr. Lafferty asked.

Jana shook her head, not wanting to get drawn into an adult conversation about sexism.

"Their eyesight," he said, tapping beside his right eye with his index finger. "The world starts slowly growing dimmer and harder to see the minute you turn forty. I should know."

"Whoa," Jana said.

"Yeah," Mr. Lafferty said. "Anyway, with that crowd, your fantastic physicality and your expressive features will be like catnip. Small actors get swallowed up in a big space, but you were built for Broadway, Jana Watson."

Chills went down her spine and she grinned at him.

"Anyway, I hope you had a great summer, and don't forget," he said and paused, waiting for her to say it.

"Own it," she replied, meaning it.

"Own it, indeed," he had agreed.

The door behind her opened again, rousing Jana from her memories.

She turned to see if Vi was ready to go.

But it was Fletcher who stood in the threshold, gazing at her like she was an ice cream sandwich on a hot summer day.

Jana felt the blood rush to her cheeks. After the dream she'd just had it was impossible to look at the handsome alien without wanting to throw herself at him.

"Good morning," Fletcher said politely.

"Good morning," she echoed.

"You are up very early," he pointed out.

He wasn't wrong. It was about five-thirty, and it felt even earlier to her.

"Vi and I are going on a stakeout," Jana told him.

"Is that like a cookout?" he asked, looking interested. "Is there steak?"

Jana suppressed a chuckle. The aliens were enormous, and they were always ready for a big meal, even a steak dinner at five-thirty in the morning.

"Not quite," Jana explained. "You know the man in town with the missing cars that we were talking about - Herman Wendall?"

"The cars that are called clunkers?" Fletcher asked.

"Yes," Jana said. "Well, we're trying to figure out who stole his old cars, and why."

"How will you do that?" Fletcher asked, sitting down across from her.

"Well, we figured it would be difficult to steal cars that aren't functional. You can't just drive them away." Jana said. "Vi did the research, and there's only one car towing company in this whole area that has a flat bed truck. So we suspect the owner may know something about the theft."

But by the time she finished explaining, she was barely registering her own words. It was just that Fletcher's eye were so blue, and so deep. She swore she could see whole galaxies spinning in them.

The back door opened again, breaking the spell.

"Hey Fletcher," Vi said, coming out to join them. "You ready, Jana?"

"Sure," Jana said, wishing she didn't feel so regretful about leaving the big alien.

Vi's phone played an ominous piano chord.

"What is that sound?" Jana asked.

"A new auto listing," Vi said, almost dropping her phone in her eagerness to get it out of her pocket and check it out. "I set up alerts on all of the local auto-sales sites, just in case anyone tried to unload any of the cars we're looking for."

Jana was riveted. This was better than any soap opera.

"It's a match," Vi reported. "But it's almost a five hour drive from here. It would take us all day."

"What do we do?" Jana asked.

Vi scowled.

"As much as I want to check out the tow truck driver, I think I should go check out this car. It's a more solid lead."

"I can still do the stakeout while you and Hannibal check out the car listing," Jana offered.

Vi looked torn.

"Seriously, I'll be fine," Jana said.

"I don't know this tow truck guy," Vi said. "He was very evasive when I called him. For all we know, he's got something to to with this. He could be dangerous. And besides, if you're there for hours, you really need back-up. Solo stake-outs are for advanced detectives."

"I'll go with you, Jana," Fletcher offered.

Jana's stomach did a little backflip at the thought, and she looked at Vi for her reaction.

2

FLETCHER

Fletcher watched as the two women exchanged a look.

He was not skilled in the more subtle ways of Earth yet. They might decide that he would not be a help on the stakeout. But he wasn't sure what he would do if Jana tried to go without him.

Vi had indicated this work might be dangerous, and the need to protect Jana overwhelmed him.

Jana was his mate - he knew it to his bones. But she seemed to deny their attraction, to deny his very existence at times.

It was confusing and pleasant at the same time, being near her, but unable to claim her without upsetting some unspoken rule.

The men from Aerie were attuned to unspoken rules. On Aerie, where they had existed as gaseous masses, there was very little privacy. Manners were everything when it came to keeping society together.

So although he did not understand why Jana didn't want

to talk about their connection, he respected her boundaries and did not push it.

They would join when the time was right. He was certain of it.

"You know what?" Vi said. "That's not a bad idea."

Jana smiled and looked down in a shy way that was the opposite of her usual confidence.

Fletcher wondered what it could mean. Was she ashamed to be happy to spend time with him?

"Go tell your brothers," Vi told Fletcher. "And grab anything you need for the day."

He nodded, then jogged upstairs to find Hannibal and Spenser draped over the sofa eating breakfast.

"Hello, brothers," Fletcher said.

"Hello, Fletcher," Hannibal said. "Do you want toaster waffles?"

Hannibal gestured at a plate on the coffee table. It looked like his brothers had toasted all the waffles in the box.

"I don't have time," Fletcher replied proudly. "I am going on a stakeout."

"Is that like a cookout?" Spenser asked, sitting up quickly. "Can you bring us back some steak?"

"No," Fletcher said. "That's what I thought, too. But really it's spying."

"Oh." Spenser sat back and took a bite of his waffle.

"Who are you spying on?" Hannibal asked suspiciously.

Fletcher didn't blame him. Spying was the opposite of good manners. Everyone knew that.

"A man who Vi suspects is involved in stealing those cars," Fletcher explained. "I am going with Jana, and you and Vi are going to look at another clue."

"We are?" Hannibal asked.

"And what am I doing?" Spenser asked in a grumpy way.

Fletcher's heart ached for his brother Spenser, who was having a harder time adjusting to this new world.

Spenser had not yet found a mate. And though he expressed happiness at his brothers' joy, it was clear that the big alien needed a mate of his own to ease his transition to Earth.

"Did you not promise to go to the garden store with Micah and Tony?" Hannibal asked Spenser.

"Oh, yes," Spenser remembered, looking more cheerful.

Tony had said the best hamburgers in town could be obtained at the restaurant next to the garden store. The three were planning to make a day of their excursion.

Fletcher ran to his room and grabbed his backpack. He looked around, uncertain what he was supposed to bring for a stakeout.

He decided on a warm sweater and a dictionary. Then he headed for the kitchen and grabbed a few snacks and two bottles of water and crammed those in as well.

Satisfied, he headed for the door.

"What will you and Jana be doing?" Hannibal asked.

"I think we sit in the car and watch for the man who owns the tow truck to appear," Fletcher said.

"So you will be doing almost nothing?" Hannibal asked. "For hours?"

"Uh, yes," Fletcher realized this was true.

"Are you going to talk to her?" Hannibal asked.

Spenser leaned forward again to see what Fletcher would say.

"I-I am not sure," Fletcher said. "I do not wish to frighten her. It seems that there is some barrier to our union."

"How do you know?" Hannibal asked. "Have you talked to her?"

He hadn't. But Jana was the best kind of human, the kind who wore her feelings plainly on her face, which made it easier for an alien to understand how a conversation was going.

The only times Jana made herself vague and unreadable were those moments when they were close enough to touch, when the electric attraction between them was undeniable.

It gave Fletcher the feeling that she was unready, or perhaps unwilling to be his mate.

And as much as he ached for her, it was more important to him that she feel happy. Her vibrant happiness was his favorite thing about her.

He would not be the one to rob her of any part of it.

"Go with your instinct, brother," Spenser said suddenly in his deep serious voice.

"I will," Fletcher told him gratefully, heading for the door.

"But don't wait so long that you make her think you don't want her." Hannibal cried out after him as he closed the door.

Thanks for reading the sample of **Fletcher!**

Want to see what happens when Jana and Fletcher are forced into close quarters for their stakeout? Want to know if they can restrain their growing desires long enough to find some clues?

Then grab your copy NOW!

Fletcher: Stargazer Alien Mystery Brides #2

https://www.tashablack.com/samysterybrides.html

TASHA BLACK STARTER LIBRARY

Packed with steamy shifters, mischievous magic, billionaire superheroes, and plenty of HEAT, the Tasha Black Starter Library is the perfect way to dive into Tasha's unique brand of Romance with Bite!

Get your FREE books now at tashablack.com!

ABOUT THE AUTHOR

Tasha Black lives in a big old Victorian in a tiny college town. She loves reading anything she can get her hands on, writing paranormal romance, and sipping pumpkin spice lattes.

Get all the latest info, and claim your FREE Tasha Black Starter Library at www.TashaBlack.com

Plus you'll get the chance for sneak peeks of upcoming titles and other cool stuff!

Keep in touch...
www.tashablack.com
authortashablack@gmail.com

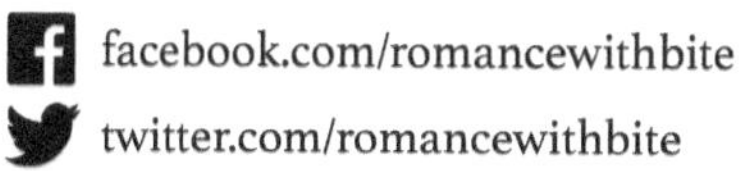

www.ingramcontent.com/pod-product-compliance
Lightning Source LLC
Chambersburg PA
CBHW030309160726
47992CB00005B/1944